"Money A..."

"That's cynical and sad," Willow said.

"That's realistic."

"You've never been married, have you?"

"I don't do relationships, remember?"

"Kane, be serious. Don't you ever want more?"

He walked toward her and crowded her against the counter. "This isn't going to work," he said. "You can prance around all you want, but it's not going to change anything."

"Prance? I don't prance."

"You move, you sway, you glide, you intrigue. But I will not be tempted. This is over. We do not have nor will we ever have a relationship. It was a great night. Maybe the best night. But it's not going to happen. I will not let you in."

Dear Reader,

The fun of THE MILLION DOLLAR CATCH series
continues with Willow's story. Willow has possibly the
worst taste in men ever. Seriously. She finds guys who
need rescuing, fixes them up and then they leave her. Not
a well-thought-out plan on her part. So when she literally
stumbles into the arms of Kane Dennison, she has no idea
what she's getting herself into.

Kane is a warrior in every sense of the word. He's dark,
he's dangerous, he's unbelievably sexy. He's also as
determined to avoid Willow as she is to be a part of his
life. But honestly, how can one powerful, wealthy, alpha
male expect to stand up against a petite, semivegetarian,
cartoonist gardener who simply won't go away? The poor
man doesn't know what hit him.

Willow is exactly what our solitary hero needs. He just
hasn't realized it yet. *The Unexpected Millionaire* is
delicious, hot, sexy fun with plenty of twists and turns. I
hope you enjoy the ride.

Susan Mallery

SUSAN MALLERY

THE UNEXPECTED MILLIONAIRE

Silhouette®

Desire

Published by Silhouette Books

America's Publisher of Contemporary Romance

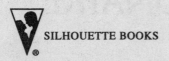 SILHOUETTE BOOKS

ISBN-13: 978-0-373-76767-0
ISBN-10:   0-373-76767-6

THE UNEXPECTED MILLIONAIRE

Copyright © 2006 by Susan Macias Redmond

This edition published by arrangement with Harlequin Books S.A.

® and TM are trademarks of Harlequin Books S.A., used under license.
Trademarks indicated with ® are registered in the United States Patent
and Trademark Office, the Canadian Trade Marks Office and in other
countries.

Visit Silhouette Books at www.eHarlequin.com

Printed in U.S.A.

Recent books by Susan Mallery

Silhouette Desire

***The Substitute Millionaire* #1760
***The Unexpected Millionaire* #1767

Silhouette Special Edition

**The Sheik & the Princess in Waiting* #1606
**The Sheik & the Princess Bride* #1647
**The Sheik & the Bride Who Said No* #1666
**The Sheik and the Virgin Secretary* #1723
†*Prodigal Son* #1729
‡*Having Her Boss's Baby* #1759
‡*The Ladies' Man* #1778

Harlequin Next

There's Always Plan B #1

*Desert Rogues
†Family Business
‡Positively Pregnant
**The Million Dollar Catch

SUSAN MALLERY

is a bestselling and award-winning author of over fifty books for Harlequin Books and Silhouette Books. She makes her home in Los Angeles with her handsome prince of a husband and her two adorable but not bright cats.

Don't miss any of the titles in Susan Mallery's series

THE MILLION DOLLAR CATCH:
Three rich, powerful men and
the ultimate wedding wager.

One

About eight seconds too late, Willow Anastasia Nelson realized there was a massive flaw in her plan.

She'd driven over to Todd Aston the Third's embarrassingly huge estate to give the slimy, no-good weasel a piece of her mind. But she'd never actually met the man, so she didn't know what, exactly, he looked like.

She had an idea, of course, sort of. Tallish, handsomeish, rich. But wasn't his hair dark and weren't his eyes brown? Why hadn't she thought to look him up on the Internet? He was probably on the front page of "JerksMonthly.com."

And if Todd Aston defined the whole tall, dark and yucky scenario, then who was the blond hunk and a half standing in front of her?

"Oh, hi," she said, smiling at the man who'd opened the front door and hoping she didn't look as out of place as she felt. "I was hoping to have a word with Todd. This is his house, right? My sister mentioned he lived here and…"

Willow groaned. That hadn't come out right. She sounded like a groupie.

"My sister knows him," she added helpfully.

Blond guy didn't step aside to let her in, although he did fold his arms over his chest in a move that got her attention. The man was *big*—really muscled, but not in a too-buff, action hero kind of way. This guy looked powerful, like a jaguar. She would bet he could snap her forearm without breaking a sweat.

His eyes were green and kind of catlike, she thought absently, continuing the whole "powerful cat" analogy. He had a good face—handsome, but also trustworthy. Not that she knew anything about him. He could be… She shook her head. She had to focus on her mission.

"Look," she said as forcefully as she could, determined to sound in charge and unintimidated by the burly guy's presence. "I need to talk to Todd. I'd like to do more, of course. He totally messed things up for my sister. Everything turned out in the end, but what if it hadn't? I get so mad when I think about it, I just want to pop his pointy little head. And that's the least of it."

The man in the doorway raised one eyebrow, then pushed aside the front of his suit jacket. Willow felt all the blood rush out of her head—no doubt fleeing to somewhere much safer than her body.

The man had a gun.

She could see it just inside his coat, tucked under his arm in some kind of holster. It was almost like in the movies, except for the cold knot of terror in her stomach.

"What is your business with Mr. Aston?" the man asked in a low voice that sent chills tripping down her spine.

So he wasn't Todd. She'd sort of guessed that, but now she knew for sure. "I, ah, he…"

The smartest move would be to leave. She wanted to yell at Todd, not get shot. But some stubborn streak made her plant her feet more firmly on the oversize and pillared porch.

"I think you're overreacting," she muttered, forcing herself to look away from the gun, back to the man threatening her with it. Well, not *threatening*, but intimidating. Something he was doing really, really well.

"I get paid to overreact."

"Has weasel-man already left for the office?" she asked sweetly. "I'll catch him there."

"You won't be catching him anywhere. Who are you and what do you want with Mr. Aston?" As he spoke, he reached out to grab her arm.

Willow had tried out every year of high school for the cheerleading squad. But in a world of amazons, she'd been too short. No matter how well she knew the routine, putting her in the lineup made them look off balance. Still, she'd been good at tumbling and turning and ducking.

The skills came back to her now as she faked a spin to the left, instead went to the right, then ducked under the big guy's arm. Suddenly she was inside the house.

Elation filled her. If Todd was here, she would find him. Then she would yell at him and her world would be set to rights.

She sprinted down the wide entryway, Mr. Big Gun and Cranky right behind her, then ran through huge rooms with soaring ceilings. This place was more like a museum than a house, she thought as she raced through what looked like a study and came out in a long hallway. She heard the man with the gun running behind her. She was fairly confident he wouldn't actually shoot her, but just in case, she wove back and forth and kept close to walls.

"Todd," she yelled as she ran. "Are you home? You need to get your lying, slimy butt down here. You don't have the right to mess with people's lives. It's wrong. You should know better."

Perhaps not words to put fear into his heart, but they would have to do.

She heard footsteps closing in and righteous anger gave her a burst of speed. Unfortunately that burst led her into a room with no other exits.

Panic energized her. She spun quickly, looking for a door, a big window, anything. Then she stared at the floor to ceiling drapes and headed in that direction.

Victory! A French door that led onto a patio as big as her elementary school had been. She burst outside and glanced around.

The grounds were stunning. The patio led to stairs that flowed into a terraced garden that reminded her of the grounds around Versailles. Beyond them was a forest of trees.

Didn't Todd know he was in the middle of Los Angeles?

"Stop," Burly Guy demanded as he ran out of the house after her. "Stop, or I'll make you stop!"

Ha! He hadn't been able to stop her yet, had he? But had he already called the police? Willow didn't wait to ask. She bolted for the trees.

Unfortunately the open ground gave her pursuer the advantage, mostly because his legs were a lot longer than hers. That combined with her erratic commitment to physical fitness and any sort of regular exercise program meant he gained on her far too quickly.

She dug down for more righteous indignation to give

her speed, or slow him down or something, but there wasn't anything left. Her breath came in pants, the sound of her rapid heartbeat filled her ears, and she felt the chilling fingers of defeat reaching for her.

"I will not be taken alive," she gasped as she surged forward, straining to reach the trees. Once there, she might have a chance. As for not being taken alive, okay, yeah, she had a slight dramatic streak.

She felt him reach for her and darted to the left, where a tree root jutted out of some grasses. She tripped over it, lost her balance and started to go down.

As she did, several things happened at once. There was an awful sensation of pain from her left ankle, she saw something gray and white and furry in a hollowed-out base of the tree, and what felt like a tank plowed into her from the rear.

She hit the ground, all the air rushed out of her lungs, and there were actual spinning lights where the rest of the world should have been.

She resurfaced to someone rolling her onto her back and telling her to take a breath.

Breath? She couldn't breathe. She really was not going to get out of here alive. Oh, God—she'd been kidding. She didn't want to die here. Now. Like this.

"Take a breath," the man repeated. "You're fine."

How did he know that? How could he be sure?

Willow opened her mouth and sucked in air. It filled her lungs. She did it again and again until the lights faded and she could focus on everything around her.

Gun Guy sat next to her. He'd removed his jacket. The good news was she could see he was all muscle and it was pretty impressive. The bad news was his gun was totally exposed and she couldn't pretend it wasn't there.

"Who *are* you?" he asked. "Some crazy ex-girlfriend? I usually know them, but every now and then…"

Willow raised herself up on one elbow. "Ex-girlfriend? No way. I wouldn't date Todd if the continuation of the entire planet depended on it. Well, okay, if it would save some endangered species, maybe. We all have to do our part. It's important for us to realize that for the planet to continue to be a renewable resource, there are some basic rules we need to follow."

He held up his hands in the shape of a T. "Time-out. Who are you?" he asked again.

"Oh. Sorry. Willow. My sister is Julie Nelson. She's engaged to Ryan, Todd's cousin. But rat fink Todd did everything he could to keep them apart and I can't let that go. I know I should just accept it and move on, but it was wrong. He thinks because he's so rich, he's king of the world or something. Idiot. Who are you?"

"Kane Dennison. I'm in charge of security."

"Here at the house?"

His expression hardened, as if she'd just insulted him. "For the entire company."

"Oh, sure. That explains the gun." She pushed herself into a sitting position and brushed at the grass stains on her sweater. "I wasn't going to hurt him, you know. I mean come on, look at me. Do I look dangerous? Seriously?"

He tilted his head as if considering the question. "You're short and scrawny, so I guess not."

The short she could handle—it was a reality she couldn't change. But scrawny?

"Excuse me? I'm petite."

"Is that what they call it?"

"I have curves," she said, really annoyed and just a little hurt. Maybe she didn't have big curves or a lot of them, but they were there. "It's the sweater. It's bulky, so you can't see what's underneath, but I'm very sexy."

She wasn't—not really. She tried, of course. But it was a losing cause. Still, to have this man just dismiss her like that was more than annoying.

"I'm sure you're stunning," Kane muttered, suddenly looking as if he wished he were anywhere but here. "I'm sorry you're mad at Todd, but you can't show up at the man's house and threaten him. It's wrong and it's illegal."

"Really?" She'd broken the law? "Are you going to have me arrested?"

"Not if you leave quietly and never come back."

"But I *have* to talk to him. It's just one of those things. He needs a good talking to."

One corner of Kane's mouth turned up. "You think you can scare him?"

"Maybe." Although in truth she'd kind of lost her passion for the job. "I could come back later."

"I'm sure Todd would be delighted to hear that. You have a car?"

"What?" she asked. "Of course I have a car."

"Then let's get you to it and we'll pretend this never happened."

A course of action that made sense. There were only a couple of problems standing in the way. Standing, or not standing being the main one.

"I can't," she said and rotated her foot. Instantly pain shot through her ankle and made her clench her teeth. "I think I broke my ankle when I fell."

Kane muttered something under his breath and shifted so that he was by her foot. He lifted it gently and held it in one hand while untying the laces with the other.

She wore size six shoes, which, considering she was

only five foot three, wasn't all that dainty. Still, his large hand nearly dwarfed her foot. Wasn't there some old wives' tale about guys and big hands?

Willow didn't know whether to laugh or blush at the thought, so she let it go and watched him carefully remove her athletic shoe.

"Move your toes," he said.

She did. The pain made her wince.

He peeled off her sock and began to examine her foot. Willow winced again, but this time it had nothing to do with pain. Even with her total lack of medical training, she could see her ankle swelling.

"That can't be good," she murmured. "I'm going to walk with a limp for the rest of my life."

He looked at her. "You sprained your ankle. You'll need to rest it and ice it for a couple of days, then you'll be fine."

"How do you know?"

"I've seen enough sprains."

"There's a lot of that in the security business? You work with especially clumsy people?"

He drew in a long breath. "I just know, okay?"

"Hey, I'm the one with the potentially life-threatening injury here. If anyone gets an attitude, it's me."

He muttered something that sounded like "Why me?" then he moved next to her and before she realized what was happening, picked her up in his arms.

The last time Willow had been carried anywhere, she'd been seven and throwing up from too much junk at the county fair. She shrieked and wrapped her arms around Kane's neck.

"What are you doing?" she demanded. "Put me down."

"I'm taking you inside so we can ice your ankle. Then I'll wrap it and figure out a way to get you home."

"I can drive."

"I don't think so."

"You said it wasn't that bad," she reminded him as she noticed he seemed to carry her effortlessly. Apparently the muscles were for real.

"You're in some kind of shock. You shouldn't be driving."

Shock or not, she didn't like the sensation of being swept away. She preferred to be in charge of her own destiny. Besides, there were other considerations.

"You left my shoe and sock back there," she said. "And your jacket."

"I'll get them when you're settled."

"What about the cat?"

Her rescuer gave her a look that told her he was questioning her grip on reality. She really hated when that happened.

"The one in the tree. I think she's giving birth. I saw her when I was falling—I'm good at multitasking that way. It's cold. We can't leave her out there. Do you have a box and some old towels? Or newspaper first, maybe towels later. Isn't birth messy? I know it's a part of the cycle of life and all, but there are fluids."

He stepped onto the stone path and walked toward a gatehouse. Willow let the cat issue drop as she stared at the pretty structure. It was all windows and wood, perfectly suited for the surroundings. But it wasn't the main house.

"Hey, where are you taking me?" she demanded, having sudden visions of a dark dungeon with chains and handcuffs on the walls.

"My house. I have first-aid supplies here."

Oh, right. That made sense. "You live on the property?"

"It's convenient."

"It shortens the commute, if nothing else." She glanced around at the gardens. "Nice southern exposure. You could grow anything here." Gardening was a favorite hobby. Her fingers itched to be in the soil and planting.

"If you say so."

He slowly lowered her to the ground, but kept an arm around her and supported most of her weight. She leaned on him, her body nestled close.

He had to be well over six feet and a couple hundred pounds. He felt as solid as a building and she had the thought that whatever happened, this was a man who could keep a woman safe.

He dug keys out of his trouser pocket, then unlocked the door and carried her inside.

"If we were dating, this would be romantic," she said with a sigh. "Can we pretend?"

"To be dating? No."

"But I'm injured. I may die and, frankly, it's your fault. Is it because you're married?"

He lowered her into the chair by the fireplace, then put her injured foot on the ottoman.

"You're the one who ran," he said. "It's your fault. I'm not married and don't move."

He disappeared into what Willow suspected was the kitchen. All right, so Kane didn't mind doing the rescue thing, but he wasn't exactly friendly about it. She could handle that.

She looked at the room, liking the high beamed ceiling and the earth tones. The space was bigger than she would have thought, yet still cozy. The large windows that faced south cried out for a few planter boxes, though.

On the table next to her was a book on the Middle East. Financial magazines littered the coffee table in front of the sofa. Interesting reading for a security guy.

"Engaged?" she yelled.

He mumbled something she couldn't hear, then said, "No."

"So the lack of pretending is a personal thing. Are you getting ice?"

"Yes."

"Don't forget the box for the cat."

"There's no cat."

"Oh, there's a cat. It's too cold. Even if she'd be okay, what about her kittens? They're newborn. We can't just leave them to die."

"There's no damn cat."

There was a cat, Kane thought grimly as he stared into the hollow of the tree. A gray and white one with three tiny kittens. Despite having been pregnant until a couple of hours ago, the cat looked skinny and bedraggled.

A stray, he thought, wondering what he'd done to deserve this. He was a decent guy. He tried to do the right thing. All he asked was that the world leave him alone. For the most part, the world agreed. Until today.

As the odds of the cat getting into the box were close to zero, he set it on the ground and studied the situation. He wasn't a pet person, but he knew enough to know cats had claws, teeth and miserable dispositions. However, this cat had recently given birth, so maybe it was weak and therefore feeling more cooperative. It was also a new mother and likely to be protective.

One way or the other, he knew there was going to be blood spilt and it was going to be his.

He reached inside the hollow and closed his hand around the first kitten. The mother cat stared at him and put her paw on top of his hand. As he began to move the impossibly small ratlike baby, claws sank into his skin. Oh, yeah, a real good time.

"Look. I've got to get you and the kittens inside. It's cold and it'll be foggy tonight. I know you're hungry and tired so just shut up and cooperate."

The cat blinked slowly. The claws retracted.

He scooped up the kittens and set them in the nest of towels he'd folded in the box, then reached for the mother cat. She hissed, then rose and jumped gracefully onto the towels and curled up around her babies.

Kane grabbed his coat, Willow's shoe and sock and the box, then headed back to his place.

This wasn't how his day was supposed to go. He lived a quiet life by choice. He liked his place—it was secluded and he didn't get visitors. Solitude was his friend and he didn't need any others. So why did he have an uncomfortable sensation that everything was about to change?

He walked into the gatehouse and found Willow on the phone.

"Gotta go," she said. "Kane's back with the cat and her kittens. Uh-huh. No, that's great. Thanks, Marina. I appreciate it."

"You called someone?" he asked as he set the box by the fireplace.

"You gave me the phone. Was I not supposed to use it?"

"It was for emergencies."

"You didn't say that. Anyway, the call was local. I phoned my sister. She's bringing over cat food and a litter box. Oh, and some dishes, because I didn't think you'd want to use yours for the cat food. I'd put money on her calling Mom and telling her what happened, which means Dr. Greenberg is probably going to want to check me out before I can move."

"You have a doctor who makes house calls?"

"My mom's worked for him for years. He's great." She glanced at her watch. "We should have this all wrapped up by two or three. Really. But if you have to be somewhere, don't let me keep you."

As if he was going to leave her alone in his place. "I can work from home today."

"So that's all good."

She smiled at him, as if all this was normal. As if *she* was normal.

"You can't do this," he told her. "You can't invade my life."

"I didn't invade it. I stumbled into it. Literally."

There was that smile again—the one that transformed her from pretty to beautiful and made her eyes twinkle. As if there was a joke that only she got. Which, based on her loose grasp of reality, was probably true.

"Who the hell are you?" he demanded.

"I told you. Julie's sister."

"Why aren't you at work?"

"Oh, I work from home, too. I'm a cartoonist, actually. I have my own comic strip. I'm syndicated. Do you have anything to eat? I'm starved."

He didn't keep much food around. It was always easier to grab a meal on his way home from work. But there had to be something.

"I'll go look." He stalked toward the kitchen.

"Nothing with meat. I'm a vegetarian."

"Of course you are," he muttered.

The cat had followed him into the kitchen. He searched his bare pantry and found a can of tuna. After opening it, he dumped the contents on a plate and set it on the floor. The cat gulped down the food.

"She must have been starving."

He looked up and saw Willow standing in the doorway. She was balanced on one foot, holding on to the door frame, her gaze focused on the stray.

"Poor thing. All alone in the world and pregnant. You know whoever the guy cat is, he didn't bother to stick around. It's just so typical. A real statement on our society today."

Kane rubbed his temples as he felt the beginnings of a headache.

"You should be sitting," he said. "You need to ice your ankle."

"I'm getting cold from the ice. Do you have any tea?"

He wanted to snap back that this wasn't the kitchen at the Four Seasons and no he didn't have any damn tea. That she should be grateful he hadn't left her and the stupid cat out there to freeze to death.

Except this was Los Angeles and it never got close to freezing and there was something in Willow's blue eyes, an expectation of goodness and trust, that stopped him.

She was the kind of woman who expected the best from people and would bet a large portion of his considerable bank account that she'd been disappointed more often than not.

"No tea."

She nodded. "Not the tea type, huh? You're too macho for that."

"Macho?"

"Manly, virile, whatever."

"Virile?"

"I'm just guessing on that one. It might not be true. You don't seem to have a woman in your life."

He felt an unusual need to growl at her. "You screw with my day, threaten my boss, run from me, blame me because you tripped and now you're questioning my...my..."

"Manhood?" she offered helpfully. "Am I making you

crazy? It happens. I try not to do that to people and I don't always know when I'm doing it."

"You're doing it now."

"Then I'll stop. Would it help if I hopped back to my chair?"

"More than you know."

"Okay."

She turned, then swayed and grabbed on to the door frame to keep her balance. He swore and stepped over the cat to pick her up.

"It's just the blood loss," she said as she rested her head on his shoulder. "I'll be fine."

"Especially considering you haven't lost any blood."

"But I could have."

He turned his head to look at her. It was only then that he realized how close their mouths were. His gaze locked on the curve of her lips and he had a pressing need to rest his mouth there. Just for a second. To know what she felt like and how she tasted.

He shouldn't. He would only hurt her—it was as inevitable as the sunrise and yet he was tempted.

"I wouldn't mind," she whispered. "I know I'm not your type but I wouldn't ever tell anyone."

He didn't know what she was talking about and he didn't care. Because for once in his life, he was going to do the one thing he knew he shouldn't.

He was going to kiss her.

Two

Kane claimed Willow with a kiss that took her breath away. Powerful, sensual, erotic. She couldn't say what was different, how his mouth pressing against hers was unlike any other kiss, but it was.

His lips were firm and demanding, but with a gentleness that made her want to give him anything he wanted. She knew he could just claim her—he was more than capable of taking, but the fact that he didn't seemed to make him even more powerful and appealing.

She clung to him, her arms around his neck. Her body straining to be closer. He touched his tongue to her lower lip and she parted for him instantly.

When he swept into her mouth, she felt heat pouring through her body. Need made her quiver and if she'd been standing, she would have collapsed.

His tongue explored her, teased her, excited her. He

tasted of coffee and some exotic flavor that left her hungry for more. She kissed him back with an enthusiasm that probably should have embarrassed her, but as she figured this was a one time thing, why not go for it.

The kiss went on and on until various parts of her body began complaining that they, too, wanted some of that. Her breasts ached and between her legs she felt a distinct longing.

Finally he raised his head and looked at her. Passion darkened his eyes to the color of storm clouds, which was something she'd never been able to think before. The wanting tightened his features and made him look predatory.

"You want to have sex with me!" she announced, so pleased she nearly kissed him again.

He muttered something under his breath and carried her back to the chair on the living room.

"We're *not* having sex," he told her.

"Oh, I know. I don't know you and that would make it tacky, but you were interested. Plus, you held me for a long time without breaking a sweat. So you must work out."

He shook his head. "I've never understood why anyone would want to bang his head against a wall, but now I get it."

She ignored that. "Kane?"

He glanced at her.

Her breath caught. It was still there—the need. Men had offered to take her to bed before, but they'd never *needed* her. Not sexually.

"Wow. I'm not imagining it. You are so incredibly sweet. Thank you."

"I'm not sweet. I'm a cold son of a bitch."

Oh, please. She smiled. "You've made my whole day. Guys don't ever want me. Not really."

He looked her up and down in a blatantly sexual way.

She supposed that to be a fully realized woman, she should be insulted, but in truth, it was thrilling.

"Trust me—guys want you. You're just not paying attention."

"No, they don't. I'm the warm, caring type who takes in strays. I give them a home—well, not literally. I mean they don't come live with me. But I rescue them. You know, patch them up, give them support, care about them and then they leave. But they never…you know."

"Wanted to sleep with you?" he asked bluntly.

She winced. "Not usually. Which is fine. Some are just friends, but others…" She shrugged. "It's kind of the way my life goes."

She could deal with that—it was her destiny to fix the guys and send them on their way. But sometimes she wished they would see her as something other than a good friend. There had been a couple she'd wanted to stick around.

"Just so we're clear," he said. "I don't need rescuing."

She wasn't sure she believed him, but she was willing to let it go for now. Mostly because the wanting thing was so incredible.

"You're so good-looking and powerful," she said with a sigh. "Not my type at all, not that I'm complaining."

"Good to know," he said dryly.

"You could kiss me again. I wouldn't mind."

"While that's a pretty irresistible invitation, I'll find you something to eat instead."

She was kind of hungry. "But you do still want me, right? That hasn't faded."

He looked into her eyes and she felt the pull of his need. Her insides got all hot and quivery.

"Wow," she breathed as he turned away. "You're good."

"I live to serve."

He crossed to the kitchen where she heard him opening cupboard doors. She glanced at the mother cat licking her babies.

"I think you're going to be really happy here," she whispered. "Kane is nice and gentle. He'll be a good owner."

Or he *would* be, once she convinced him that he wanted to keep the mother cat and her kittens. He was at heart, she believed, a decent man. With her need to rescue, she didn't find decent very often.

There was a knock on the door.

"I'll get that," she said as she slid to the edge of the chair and prepared to stand on one leg.

"This is my place and I'll get it," he told her as he walked across the hardwood floor. "Sit. Stay."

"You kiss too good for me to be scared of you," she told him.

He ignored her and opened the door. "Yes?"

"I'm Marina Nelson. I'm here to see my sister." She thrust a bag into his arms. "There are more in the car."

Willow twisted in her seat and waved. "You came."

"Of course I came. You said you'd fallen and broken your ankle."

"I called Marina because I knew she was home this morning," Willow said to Kane, "Julie's at work. Are you going to step aside so she can come in?"

"I haven't decided."

"You could push past him," Willow told her sister.

Marina shook her head. "He looks burly."

Willow opened her mouth to say that he wasn't all that tough and that he was an amazing kisser, then she thought better of it. It was really the sort of information she needed to keep to herself.

"You look alike," Kane said.

Willow sighed. Obviously he was going to be difficult. "All three of us do. It's quite a gene pool. Are you going to let her in?"

"Do I have a choice?"

"If I leave now, I'll only come back with reinforcements," Marina told him.

"Right."

He moved aside and Marina slipped past him. She rushed to the chair and hugged Willow.

"What on earth happened? What are you doing here? What did you do to your poor foot?" Marina sank onto the ottoman and leaned forward. "Start at the beginning and tell me everything."

Kane took the single bag into the kitchen, then disappeared outside.

"So talk," Marina said.

"I haven't been able to forget about Todd," Willow began. "I kept getting madder and madder. Or is it more mad? Anyway, when I woke up this morning, I just couldn't stand it anymore."

Marina looked at her. "Tell me you didn't come over here to take him on."

"That's exactly what she did," Kane said as he walked in with an armful of bags. "Are there more in the trunk?"

"No, just those in the backseat. Thanks."

He grunted, then disappeared into the kitchen.

Willow watched him go, admiring the way his slacks tightened around his butt as he moved. She'd never been one of those women who admired men's rears before, but then she'd never seen one this good.

"Willow," Marina said impatiently.

"What? Oh, sorry. So I came over here to yell at Todd. He nearly broke up Julie and Ryan and I couldn't stand thinking about that. I mean who does he think he is? Plus there's the whole million dollar thing just hanging out there and he's so self-centered and egotistical you just know he's thinking we're dying to meet him now that Julie's engaged. I just want to beat him with a stick."

"For someone who's a vegetarian and so into being one with nature, you're surprisingly violent," Kane called from the kitchen.

"I'm not violent," she yelled back. "I wasn't the one flashing a gun around. Where is it, by the way?"

"Somewhere you can't get it."

Marina's eyes widened. "He had a gun?"

"Yes, but don't worry about it. So I came here and Kane answered the door and I guess he thought I was a serious threat because he tried to grab me."

"What?"

"It's his job. He's in charge of security for all of Todd and Ryan's companies. You have to be clear on that. He's a little touchy about people thinking he's only in charge of the house or something."

"I'm not touchy."

The words were a little garbled, as if he were speaking through clenched teeth.

She leaned forward and lowered her voice. "He really is. Who knew? Okay, so he tried to grab me, I ran and got through the house, but he caught up with me on the grounds. Then I tripped, and as I went down, I not only ripped off my ankle, I saw the cat there giving birth. So here we are."

Marina covered her mouth, then dropped her hand to her lap. "I swear, I don't know if I should laugh or shriek. Only you, Willow, only you."

Kane walked out of the kitchen, holding a litter box in his hand. "Is this what I think it is?"

"Only if you think it's a cat box," Marina said, then turned back to her sister. "It's completely disposable and biodegradable. Cool, huh?"

"Very. Thanks for that. Where do you think we should put it?"

Marina glanced around the living room. "Somewhere a little more private."

Kane stared from the women to the litter box and back. What the hell had happened? When had he lost control of the situation, not to mention his life?

"I'll go find a place," Marina said. She stood and took the box from him, then smiled. "It's kind of a lot to take in. You probably need a minute to recover."

He watched her walk out of the living room and down the hallway. Great, Willow thought he needed rescuing and her sister was convinced he was an idiot.

"Is there a scooper?" Willow asked him. "You'll want that by the box, along with some paper towels.

He started to ask for what, then stopped himself. Right— it was basically a cat's bathroom. There would be deposits.

"She'll know how to use it, right?" he asked as he jerked his head toward the cat.

"Oh, sure. We'll just show her where it is."

Marina returned without the litter box. "The bathroom off the second bedroom seems like a good bet. I put it there." She walked to her sister, bent over and said in a low voice, "It doesn't look like he has women here on a regular basis, so that's something."

He was equally outraged and admiring. "I'm standing right here."

Willow smiled at him. "We know."

"He seems okay," Marina continued. "But given your history with guys..."

"It's true," Willow said sadly. "Maybe he's different."

"Still standing here," he announced.

"You could feed the cat," Willow said. "You'll probably be more comfortable in the kitchen while we're talking about you behind your back."

In a scary, twisted way, her words made sense. He retreated to the kitchen, all the while wondering what had happened. This morning everything about his life had been normal and pleasantly solitary. Somewhere along the way, he'd been invaded. There were people here—he didn't do people.

He went through the bags. There was canned cat food, a bag of dry and three bowls. He filled one with water and the other with dry food. The mother cat rushed into the kitchen and fell on the food. When he dished up some canned, she abandoned the dry to feast on that.

While she ate, he checked out the rest of the bags. Marina had brought over bread, honey, several packages of frozen soup, bags of cookies, apples, pears, some girly soap and the latest issue of a celebrity gossip magazine. Did she think her sister was moving in?

He felt something brush against his leg. When he glanced down he saw the mother cat rubbing her leg against him. She looked up, purring.

Feeling awkward and stupid and like he was being taken, he bent over and patted the top of her head. She turned and rubbed her jaw against his fingers. He could feel the vibration of her purring.

He'd never been one for pets. As a kid, it was all he could do to feed himself. Plus caring about anything only made you a victim. In the army, there had always been guys who kept dogs around, but he wasn't one of them.

He straightened. He could hear Willow and Marina

talking in the living room, although he couldn't hear the words, thank God. So now what? Where did he go? This was supposed to be his house, but he suddenly felt like he didn't belong.

There was another knock on the door. Before he could say anything, Marina yelled that she was getting it. He walked into his living room in time to see an older version of Willow stepping into his house, along with a fiftysomething guy in a suit.

"Mom, you didn't have to come," Willow said. "I'm fine."

Willow's mother handed Marina a casserole, then rushed to Willow's side. "You're not fine. You hurt yourself. What was I supposed to do? Just let you lie here in pain?"

"Oh, Mom."

The man approached Kane. "I'm Dr. David Greenberg, a friend of the family."

"Kane Dennison." They shook hands.

Dr. Greenberg moved over to the ottoman. "All right, Willow, let's see what you've done."

Willow's mother moved back. Marina touched her arm. "This is Kane, Mom."

The older woman smiled at him. "Hi. Naomi Nelson. She said you carried her here and saved her life."

Willow had managed to make a number of phone calls and pass on a lot of information in the short time he'd been gone, he thought, not sure if he should punish her or be impressed.

"I don't think she was all that near death," he said.

"Mom, there are kittens," Willow said. She pointed at the box.

"Oh, they're just born."

While Naomi went to coo over the kittens, Marina murmured something about putting the casserole in the refrigerator. Kane watched as the doctor examined Willow's ankle.

"Does this hurt?" he asked as he manipulated her foot. "Does this?"

She answered his questions, then looked at Kane. He felt the impact of her gaze all the way down to his groin. Funny how Marina was similar in appearance, but nothing about her turned him on. Yet with Willow, all it took was a look.

Dr. Greenberg continued his exam for a couple more minutes, then patted her knee. "You'll live. It's a minor sprain. You have some swelling, which should go away in the next couple of days. Keep doing what you're doing. Elevation and ice. You'll be better in the morning."

"It hurts," Willow said with a soft whimper.

The doctor smiled. "I remember how badly you handle pain. You're the one who cried before I ever gave you a shot when you were little." He dug around in his case and handed her a sample pack of pills. "These will help. Take them now and then don't even think about driving until tomorrow. You're going to be out of it."

She smiled. "You've been very good to me."

"I know." He stood, bent over and kissed her cheek. "Try not to be such a klutz."

"I didn't do this on purpose."

"But you still do it."

Naomi hurried over. "Thank you so much for coming."

The doctor shrugged. "I've known them nearly all their lives. They're like my girls, too. I'm going back to the office."

"I'll be there within the hour," Naomi promised.

Both women fluttered around, bringing Willow water so she could take her pill, more ice, a snack. Kane stayed in the background, watching them move so easily through his place—as if they'd been here before. Or maybe that was the way of nurturers. They were comfortable wherever they went.

At last Marina left, leaving only Willow and her mother. Naomi beckoned him into the kitchen.

"Thank you for all your help," she began. "I'm sorry we've all invaded you like this."

"It's fine," he said, when what he was thinking was more along the lines of "you could be gone now."

"I'll just get her things and take her home."

Kane eyed the woman. She was about five-five and in decent shape, but there was no way she could carry her daughter.

"I'll do that," he said, knowing it was the only way. "You can't carry her inside."

"Oh." Naomi looked concerned. "I hadn't thought about that. With her foot and all… Can she hop?"

"Not well. Don't worry. I'll get her home."

"If you're sure…" She glanced at her watch and he knew she was thinking she had to get back to work.

"Ask Willow if she's comfortable with that arrangement," he said.

Naomi nodded, then walked back into the living room. Kane followed her and watched as Willow and her mother spoke.

"I'll be fine," Willow said, glancing at him, her blue eyes bright with anticipation and humor.

He narrowed his gaze. What the hell was she planning now?

Naomi hugged her daughter, then walked over to him and held out her hand. "You've been very kind. I don't know how to thank you."

"Not a problem."

"Good luck with the cat and her kittens. They're going to be a handful."

As they wouldn't still be here while they were growing up, he didn't care.

Then she was gone and he was alone with Willow.

"Sorry about everyone coming by," she said.

"No, you're not. You invited them all. You wanted them to come."

"Okay. Maybe. I had to be sure I wasn't dying."

"Sprained ankles are rarely fatal."

"At least they brought food." She smiled. "You like food."

"How do you know?"

"You're a guy. It's a guy thing."

"I'm going to get the cat food," he said and turned back to the kitchen.

"You haven't fed her yet?" Willow sounded outraged.

He held in a groan. "Of course I fed the cat. I'm going to collect the food so you can have it."

"I don't eat cat food."

She was doing this on purpose. He knew that. She thought baiting him was a fun, new game.

"It's for the cat," he said patiently.

"The cat's not coming home with me. My building doesn't allow pets, which is one of the reasons I rented there. That and the amazing backyard. I turned it into a garden and it's so beautiful. But there are a lot of plants that would be poisonous to a kitten. Not that I wouldn't love one. But I know better. If I rescue one cat, soon I'll want to rescue them all. Then there are dogs and birds and it could really turn into a disaster."

He rarely got headaches, but he could feel one coming on.

"I'm *not* keeping the cat."

"You have to," she told him. "The kittens are too young

to be moved. They have to be warm and they need their mom. Oh, do you have a hot water bottle to put in the box, because that would be great."

He could hear a strange buzzing in his ears. "Aren't there rescue places?"

"Sure, but they're already busy with real strays. This cat has a home, at least until the babies are older."

"They don't have a home here."

She stared at him, wide-eyed. He knew he was being manipulated and knew he wasn't going to give in.

"I don't do cats," he said firmly. "Not this one, not any one."

"That's so mean."

She spoke softly. He barely heard the words, yet it was as if she'd slapped him. Her blue eyes darkened with disappointment and she seemed to shrink into the chair.

"All right," she told him. "Just get the cat supplies together. I'll figure out something."

He'd led men into more dangerous parts of the world than most people knew about. He'd killed to stay alive and had been left for dead more than once. Yet never had he felt so out of his element than he did at this moment.

What the hell did he care what this woman thought of him? It was a damn cat. Let her take it.

He went into the kitchen and put the food into a grocery bag, then carried it into the living room. But when he glanced at Willow, he saw she'd fallen asleep.

Her head lay on the armrest, her long blond hair a contrast to the dark leather. One leg curled up under her while the other one was stretched out, ice still strapped to her injured ankle.

"Willow?"

She didn't stir. In addition to being a wimp about pain,

she was also a lightweight when it came to painkillers. No wonder the doctor had told her not to drive after taking it.

The room was silent, except for the quiet purring of the mother cat and loud thudding of his own heart.

Willow woke up and had no idea where she was. As if that had never happened to her before, she immediately sat up and thought about panicking. But before the adrenaline could really get pumping, she remembered the whole Kane-ankle-cat thing and decided she was probably still in his house.

A quick glance at the clock on the nightstand told her it was nearly midnight. Wow—that pill had knocked her out for hours. She sat up and looked around. A night-light from the bathroom allowed her to see the shapes of the furniture, including the bed she'd slept on. The guest room, she thought, noting the bed wasn't huge and the furniture looked more neutral than masculine. Too bad. She really wouldn't have minded waking up in his bed…with him.

Smiling at the thought, she looked down at herself and saw that except for her shoes, she was completely dressed. Kane had been a gentleman. Wasn't that just her luck?

Willow sighed. She was never really like this about guys. But there was just something about Kane that got to her and made her want to be wild. Maybe because being around him felt safe. As if no matter what she did or how she acted, nothing bad would happen to her. He would be there, protecting her.

No one had ever been safe before.

She swung her feet over the side of the bed and stood carefully. While her ankle was still sore, it was a ton better. She could almost walk normally.

After visiting the bathroom—where she found a brand-new toothbrush and toothpaste conveniently waiting—she made use of the facilities, washed her face, brushed her teeth, then went in search of her host.

Kane was in the living room, reading. He glanced up as she entered.

"Sorry," she said. "The pill knocked me out."

"I noticed."

"So, you, um, carried me to bed."

"Yes."

"I slept through that."

"Apparently."

"You kept my clothes on."

"It seemed the polite thing to do."

"Okay."

One corner of his mouth twitched. "Should I have stripped you naked and taken you while you were unconscious?"

"Of course not. It's just…"

He kissed her before. Hadn't he meant it?

He stood and walked over to her. In less than a second, the humor was gone and he looked…predatory.

"You're playing a dangerous game," he told her. "You don't know anything about me."

It was true. The sensible part of her brain told her to quietly back away, retreat to the guest room and lock the door behind her. Only, he'd wanted her before. Really wanted her. The sensible part of her brain needed to remember how rare that was.

He reached up and fingered a strand of her hair. "Like silk," he murmured.

And then it was back—the fire that had thrilled her so much. She felt the heat burn between them, drawing her closer, making her promises, tempting her into the path of possible destruction.

Three

"I don't get it," Willow said. "I'm not your type."

"You said that before. How do you know?"

"I'm not anyone's type."

Kane shook his head. "I don't believe that."

"It's true. I have the sad, painful romantic history to prove it. I'm the best friend, the one guys confide in."

"I don't confide in anyone," he told her.

"You should. It's very healthy. Sharing problems make them seem more manageable."

"You know this how?"

"I read it in a magazine somewhere. You can learn a lot from magazines."

His dark gaze never left her face. "Go back to bed. I'll take you home in the morning."

No! She didn't want to be sent to bed like a child. "But then where will you sleep?"

"You're in the guest room. I still have my own bed."

"See, that was flirting. I was flirting. Wouldn't it be nice if you just went with it?"

He moved so fast, he was like a human blur. One second he was several feet away and the next he was right in front of her, one hand on her waist, the other wrapped around her hair. He eased forward that last inch, so they were touching everywhere.

She had the feeling he was trying to intimidate her and it would have worked, except she couldn't seem to be afraid of him.

"You won't hurt me," she whispered.

"Your faith is foolish and misplaced. You don't know what I'll do."

He bent his head and claimed her with a hard, demanding kiss. He pushed into her mouth and stroked her tongue, then sucked on her lower lip.

She wrapped one arm around his neck and gave as good as she got, stealing into his mouth and dueling right back. She felt him stiffen with surprise. He pulled her hard against him and she went willingly. The hand holding her hair tightened, drawing her head back.

He broke the kiss and stared into her eyes.

"I am dark and dangerous and I don't play the games you know," he said. "I'm not anyone you want to get involved with. I'm not nice, I don't call the next day and I'm never interested in more than a single night. You can't fix me, reform me, heal me or change me. You are so far out of your league, you don't know enough to run scared, but you should. Trust me on that."

His words made her tremble.

"I can't be afraid of you," she told him again.

"Why the hell not?"

She smiled and rubbed her index finger against his lower lip. "I'll agree that you're tough and you probably scare other people, but Kane, you rescued me and kittens and you were nice to my mom and my sister and when you put me to bed, you didn't even think about taking advantage of me. What's not to like?"

He closed his eyes and groaned. She had a feeling the sound wasn't about being turned on.

He opened his eyes. "You're impossible."

"I've heard that before."

"You're just about irresistible."

She sighed. "That's a new one. Can you say it again?"

He backed her up until she was trapped between him and the wall. She felt his body—and his arousal—pressing against her.

"I want you," he said in a low growl. "I want you naked and begging and desperate. I want to bury myself inside of you until you forget who you are. But you're a fool if you take me up on that. This is not a fun trip to the dark side. If you expect anything of me, you *will* be hurt. I'm going to walk away, Willow. I can walk away now or later. It's your choice."

She saw the truth reflected in his eyes. Once again the sensible part of her brain pointed out that the guest room was the best option. Only Willow had never met anyone like Kane before and she was unlikely to ever again. He claimed to be incredibly tough and maybe he was, but she had a feeling there was more to him than he wanted her to see.

Walk away? Not possible. Maybe he would hurt her, but maybe he wouldn't. She was willing to take the risk. She had to. There was something about him that called to her.

Besides, the guy could make her quiver with just a look.

"For a man so intent on insisting he doesn't care, you're

going out of your way to warn me off," she said. "Maybe you should stop talking and kiss me instead."

"Willow."

"See? You're doing it again. I understand the rules, I'm willing to play by them and you're still talking. You know what? I think it's all an act. I don't think you have any real intention of doing anything at all. I think—"

He grabbed her and kissed her. There were no preliminaries, just him wrapping his arms around her as he claimed her mouth with his own. He kissed her deeply, passionately, with no pause for breath or social niceties. He took, sweeping past her lips to stroke her tongue, circling her, claiming her. His possessive acts thrilled her and she freed her arms so she could hang on for the ride.

There was no fear, she thought as her body heated and her muscles lost their ability to support her. However much he threatened, he still held her gently. His hands moved up and down her back, exploring her, touching her, but there was nothing harsh about the contact.

She put her hands on his shoulders and leaned into him. His body supported hers. The combination of hard muscles and warmth thrilled her. She tilted her head and closed her lips around his tongue so she could suck.

He stiffened, then took a step back and stared at her. There was shock, pleasure and need in his eyes—an irresistible combination.

"I don't scare easily," she said with a shrug.

He shook his head, then bent down, gathered her in his arms and carried her down the hall.

They moved into a bedroom illuminated by a single lamp on a nightstand. Here the design was totally masculine with large pieces of dark furniture lining the walls. The bed could sleep twenty, and suited Kane completely.

He set her on the mattress and looked at her.

She felt the challenge of his gaze and refused to look away—even when he began unfastening the shirt he wore. When he'd removed that, he pulled off a T-shirt, exposing his bare chest.

Her breath caught. He was as muscled as she'd first thought, but there were also scars…dozens of them. Small irregular circles and long, jagged lines. Scars from surgeries and from wounds that made her ache inside.

What had happened to this man? Who had hurt him and why?

But there was no time for questions. He pulled off his loafers, then his socks. Trousers quickly followed, along with dark briefs.

And then he was naked. Beautiful and hard and ready. His body should be immortalized in marble, she thought. A master should sculpt him. Not that Kane would ever agree to pose.

He put his hands on his hips and stared at her. "You can still run," he told her.

"Not with my ankle."

"You know what I mean."

"Yes, I do. And I'm not going anywhere."

He took a step toward the bed, then stopped. "Dammit, Willow," he began.

She pulled her sweater up and over her head, then tossed it onto the floor. "So what, exactly, does a girl have to do to get your attention?"

He made a sound in his throat that was part growl, part groan. Then he was on the bed, on top of her, rolling with her so that she ended up sprawled across him. He tangled one hand in her hair and claimed her with a kiss that made her toes curl.

She parted for him, welcomed him. Their tongues danced. He stroked her bare back, his fingers moving slowly over her skin. When he reached the waistband of her jeans, he slipped his hands over the curve of her rear and squeezed.

She could feel his arousal pressing into his stomach. Her skin was hot and hungry for his touch. She wanted his hands everywhere, touching her, taking her, claiming her.

He shifted so she was on her back. His dark eyes stared into hers.

"You are so beautiful," he whispered before reaching behind her to unfasten her bra.

His words delighted her, but they weren't nearly as thrilling as his mouth on her bare breast. One moment there was fabric, then a whisper of cool air followed by the warm, wet sensation of lips and tongue.

He suckled her and she felt the pull through her belly and between her legs. His teeth scraped her nipple, then he licked that tight point until she felt a scream building up inside of her.

The wanting grew until it was unbearable. Her legs moved restlessly. She wanted to rip off the rest of her clothes and feel their naked bodies press together.

He turned his attention to her other breast and repeated his attentions. She stroked his shoulders, his back, then ran her fingers through his short hair. Sensations swept through her. Pleasure and tension and a deep hunger for more and more and more.

He began to drift lower, kissing her ribs, then her belly. He unfastened her jeans and continued to kiss as he went. Soft kisses, wet kisses, nibbling kisses. He anointed her with his mouth and tongue, driving her need higher and higher.

He grabbed the waistband of her jeans and drew them off in one easy, practiced movement. Her bikini panties went with them, leaving her as naked as he. Then he continued kissing his way down and down and down.

When he was inches from the promised land and she thought she might die if he didn't finally touch her *there*, she eased her thighs open and braced herself for the assault.

It was amazing. Hot and wet and fast and slow and everything in between. He licked all of her, teased her, made her whimper with gentle sucking before settling down into a rhythm designed to make her beg for him to never stop.

He moved his tongue back and forth, drawing her in deeper, pushing her to the edge, then pulling her back. Twice she was sure she was going to come, then he slowed and she lost it.

Her breath came in quick pants. She clutched at the sheets and dug her heels into the mattress. He picked up the pace again and she found herself straining toward her release. His tongue moved back and forth, taking her higher and higher. She was so close…so incredibly close.

"Kane," she breathed.

He stopped. He actually stopped. She felt her release slipping away and nearly cried in frustration. Then he pushed a single finger inside of her. In and out, circling. A deep, pulsing began building through her body, the intensity stunning her. She could barely breathe from all the powerful sensations. He put his mouth on her most swollen, sensitive spot and sucked. At the same time, he touched her with the very tip of his tongue.

Without warning, she exploded into her release. One second there was nothing, the next, her whole body was shaking from the powerful waves crashing through her. It was incredible and nearly violent and unlike anything she'd experienced.

The pleasure seemed to go on forever. Finally it began to fade and he raised his head to look at her.

There was still hunger in those dark eyes, but also satisfaction. She couldn't find it in her heart to even mind. The man had earned it.

"I'm boneless," she whispered.

"That was the point."

"You're really good at that."

"You're easy."

She smiled. "Words every woman longs to hear."

He knelt between her legs and reached for the nightstand drawer. "You're sexually responsive."

"Better."

He pulled out a condom, put it on and then eased between her thighs. His dark eyes were bright with wanting and need and desire. Willow reached down to guide him inside of her, then gasped as he filled her, stretching her with his hard thickness.

But instead of thrusting inside and having his way with her, he moved slowly, giving her time to adjust and appreciate their differences.

She tightened around him, wanting the experience to be as good for him as it had been for her. He groaned in appreciation, then shifted so he could touch her while he continued to move in and out.

She opened her eyes and prepared to ask him what he was doing, only at that exact moment, his fingers came in contact with her center.

She was already sensitive from what he'd done before and the combination of his skilled touch and his arousal pushing into her quickly took her to the edge of another release. She'd planned to focus on him and his pleasure, but soon it was all she could do to keep breathing.

He rubbed faster and faster, keeping the exact amount of pressure, while the pace of him moving in and out remained steady.

There was too much going on, she thought frantically. She didn't know where to focus her attention. It was all so good, so incredible, so...

Her release swept through her, making her body burn as it shuddered in waves of perfect pleasure. Kane leaned forward so he could brace himself above her and began to pump his hips. The movement was enough to keep her own climax going on and on, seemingly endless.

Nothing had ever been like this. She hadn't known her body was capable of these kinds of sensations. She clung to him, giving herself up to him, feeling him get closer and closer until he groaned and was still.

Willow tried to catch her breath. If she'd been boneless before, she was positively two-dimensional now. She would never be able to walk again, but that was okay. She would have the memories of this night to sustain her.

He rolled off her onto his back, then wrapped an arm around her and pulled her close.

She snuggled up against him and rested her head on his shoulder. She could feel the rapid beat of his heart and his heavy breathing.

"Not bad for a rookie," she said.

He laughed. "Gee, thanks."

She smiled. "You know your stuff. You could probably heal a few diseases with that technique."

"Like I said, you're easy."

If being easy meant feeling like this, she was all for it. Until tonight she'd been able to count her physical experiences on two fingers. Neither encounter had prepared her for Kane's mastery.

His heartbeat had slowed, as had his breathing. She could feel herself getting sleepy. The part of her brain that could still function wondered if she should offer to head back to the guest room bed. But then she reminded herself this was Kane. If he wanted her gone, he would have no problem telling her exactly that.

So much for being a big, bad tough guy, she thought as she snuggled closer and closed her eyes.

Kane woke shortly before dawn and knew there were two things wrong—the woman in his bed and the intruder moving through his bedroom.

He knew the woman was Willow and someone he could deal with later. First there was the matter of the intruder. But before he could slip out of bed and attack, a skinny cat jumped on his chest and meowed in his face.

"Good morning to you, too," he muttered and raised his hand. She rubbed against his fingers before settling down on his chest and purring loudly.

He shifted her onto the bed and got up. After grabbing a robe, he walked into the kitchen and started the coffee machine. The cat followed. When he'd flipped on the machine, he checked out her food. The bowl of canned was licked clean and most of the dry was gone. He gave her more of both, then walked into the living room.

The kittens were still in their box. One was awake and mewing for its mother. He bent over and stroked the tiny body. The kittens were blind and defenseless. In the wild, they'd be dead within hours. There were plenty of small predators on the grounds to deal with them. It was just the ugly side of life.

He could see that and accept it, but not Willow. She wanted to save the world. Funny how she hadn't learned that a lot of the world wasn't worth saving.

Willow awoke to sunlight spilling into the bedroom and the smell of coffee filling the house. A quick glance at the clock on the nightstand told her it was after eight and she was still in Kane's bed. Not to mention…naked.

She smiled as she stretched, feeling sore muscles protest. It had been some workout. Make that workouts with an *S*, because sometime well after three in the morning, Kane had done the whole thing again.

She stood and strolled into the bathroom where she found her clothes all neatly folded. After showering, she dressed and was able to get her foot in her shoe with no problem. The swelling was nearly gone and her ankle barely hurt at all. She walked into the kitchen and poured herself coffee, then headed for the living room.

Kane sat at a desk in the corner, facing his laptop. He, too, had showered and dressed, mostly likely in the guest room because she hadn't heard him.

He looked up at her, but didn't speak. He looked dark and dangerous and there wasn't a hint of desire or softness in his eyes.

"Don't panic," she said with a smile. "I'm leaving as soon as I'm done with my coffee, so you can afford to be pleasant. I promise, you won't have to resort to scaring me off."

"Why should I believe you? You settle in very easily."

His voice was familiar and sexy. She liked the way it played in her mind, the low notes making her shiver.

"I have things to do," she told him. "Important things."

"I can only imagine."

She walked closer to the desk. "What are you doing? Work stuff?"

"I finished that earlier. This is personal."

"Ooh. An online girlfriend."

He shook his head and turned the computer toward her. She saw a picture of a beautiful island. The sky was an impossible shade of blue, the sands nearly white. In her next life, when she was rich, she would hang out in places like that.

"Vacation?" she asked.

"Retirement. I'll be ready in eight years. Five if my investments continue to pay off better than I expect."

Retire? She frowned. "But you're barely in your thirties."

"Thirty-three."

She sank into the club chair by the desk. "Why would you want to retire?"

"Because I can. I've done as much as I want to do."

And she'd barely started on *her* life. "Like what?"

He leaned back in his chair. "I lied about my age, faked a birth certificate and joined the army when I was sixteen. I was there for ten years, eight of them in Special Forces."

Which explained the scars, she thought. A warrior. Her heart gave a little shimmy.

"After I got out, I spent four years protecting rich people in dangerous parts of the world. The money was good, but I got tired of being shot at. I took the job with Todd and Ryan because I get in on the ground floor with a lot of start-ups. It's a good way to make a fortune."

"Is that what you need? A fortune?" If he was planning on retiring in five to eight years, he probably already had one.

"I need several."

"For what?"

He jerked his head at the computer screen. "Privacy and solitude don't come cheap. I want a place that's isolated and easy to defend. Where there aren't many people but there are things I like to do."

While she could respect the desire for a fortune or two—frankly, a third of a fortune would be enough for her—she didn't understand the need to be alone.

"What about family?" she asked. "A wife, kids? You can't keep them isolated."

"Not interested."

She tightened her grip on her coffee. "But then you'll be alone."

"Exactly."

"But that's not a good thing."

He looked at her. "I told you, Willow. I don't get involved. Ever."

It was like he was speaking a foreign language. "But family is everything to me," she told him. "I'd be lost without them. Everyone needs to belong, even you."

"You're wrong."

He spoke with a confidence that made her want to believe him. But she couldn't get her mind around the fact that he was planning to spend the rest of his life by himself.

"Last night was so intimate," she murmured.

"It was sex."

"Is that the only way you feel comfortable connecting? Sexually?"

He looked more amused than annoyed. "Don't try to analyze me. It won't work. I'm not broken—I don't need fixing."

"You need more in your life than just you, Kane." But he wasn't going to believe her. She looked across the room toward the basket where the mother cat licked her kittens. "Do you want me to call the rescue place about the cats?"

"They can stay for a couple of weeks. I looked online

and by then they'll have their eyes open and be moving around. I'll take them in after that."

She wanted to take heart in the fact that he was accepting pets into his life, but she knew he meant what he said. That it was only temporary.

"Do you, ah, want help with them?" she asked. "I can come by and feed them and stuff."

"I'm good."

There was something about his tone more than his words that made her feel as if he were slipping away. As if the connection had ceased to exist between them.

"Do you mind if I come visit them before you take them to the rescue place?" she asked.

"That would be fine."

She wanted to think he meant something significant by that, but somehow she couldn't convince herself. "Okay, then I should be going."

"I moved your car around back," he said, returning his attention to the computer screen. "It's just outside the front door."

"Thanks."

She took the coffee cup back into the kitchen and rinsed it out. After collecting her purse, she walked to the front door. "I guess I'll see you around."

"Goodbye, Willow."

"Bye." She opened the door, then hesitated. "Do you want my phone number?"

He looked at her then, his dark gaze locking with hers. She searched for some hint of the fire she'd seen before, but it was so gone, it was as if it had never been.

"No, you don't," she whispered, and left.

Four

Kane finished his presentation on security for the company's latest acquisition. Todd and Ryan glanced at each other.

"Remind us not to get involved with anything this proprietary again," Ryan said. "It's a real pain."

Kane thought about the executive detail he'd had to protect for two months in Afghanistan. Compared to that, this was something he could do with his eyes closed. "It's not that difficult. I'll handle it. As long as everyone follows procedure, we're protected."

"And if they don't?" Todd asked with a grin.

"Then they answer to me," Kane said.

Todd looked at Ryan. "This is why I like him."

"Right back at you."

Todd turned back to Kane. "I heard there was some trouble at the house yesterday. I go away for one day and all hell breaks loose?"

Kane had a sudden image of Willow in his bed, her body flushed, her eyes glazed and her long, blond hair spread out on the pillow. His groin tightened, but he ignored the flash of need, not to mention the pictures in his brain. It had happened, it was over, end of story.

Still, he couldn't stop wondering why she'd wanted to be with him. He would bet a large portion of his considerable bank account that she was the type who led with her heart. So why take on a guy just for the night?

"It was Willow," Ryan said. "Julie told me last evening. Apparently Willow's still a little annoyed that you got between me and Julie."

Todd grimaced. "I didn't get between you. I was looking out for a friend. You're happy now—that's the end of it." He returned his attention to Kane. "Should I be worried?"

Kane held in a smile. "I think you could take her."

"That's not what I meant. Is she crazy?"

"No. She wanted to tell you off because you'd messed with her sister."

"It's the money," Todd grumbled. "If Aunt Ruth hadn't offered her granddaughters a million dollars to marry me, none of this would have happened."

Kane raised his eyebrows. "I didn't know you were looking for a wife."

"I'm not." Todd sighed. "Aunt Ruth is our late uncle's second wife, so we're not actually related. Ruth had a daughter who ran off when she was seventeen and got married. Ruth and our uncle cut her off and apparently never had anything to do with her until a few months ago. Our uncle died. Ruth missed her daughter and got in touch with her only to discover there were three granddaughters she'd never met. Somewhere along the way, she got it in her head that life would be perfect if one of her granddaughters married me. She offered them each a million dollars if one of them would take me on."

Todd glared at Ryan. "Do you know how insulting that is? The assumption she has to pay someone to marry me?"

Ryan grinned. "Actually it's kind of funny."

"So says the man who's getting married."

Ryan turned to Kane. "I went on the first date to throw the sisters off the path. I met Julie and after a few complications, we got engaged."

Kane knew that Julie was also pregnant, but he wasn't about to say anything. Being in charge of security meant keeping secrets—and he was good at that.

"So everything worked out," Todd said. "Willow should just let it go."

"I don't think she'll be back," Kane told him. "Although there were a few interesting events." He explained about Willow running through the grounds and spraining her ankle. He left out the cat, the kittens and the sex.

Both his bosses stared at him. "You didn't just leave her there, did you?" Todd asked.

"I took her home and iced her ankle."

"To your house," Ryan confirmed.

"Uh-huh."

"You don't usually invite people to your house," Todd said.

"I didn't invite Willow. It just happened." Which was true. If only he had an excuse for what he'd done last night…and again this morning.

She'd been a hell of a temptation, but he'd been tempted before. And resisted. There was just something about her…

"Be careful," Ryan said with a grin. "The Nelson women are complicated. Just when you least expect it, they've invaded your world and changed everything."

"I'm not worried," Todd said confidently. "I'm not

marrying either one of them. They'll have to find their million dollars elsewhere."

"I was thinking more of Kane," Ryan said with a grin. "Willow's a pretty lady."

Todd looked at Kane. "Intrigued?"

Not in the way they meant. "I don't do relationships. Don't worry about me."

She was gone and he would never see her again, which was exactly how he liked things. But as the day wore on, he found himself remembering her smile, her laugh and the way she'd felt in his arms. It was as if she were a song he couldn't shake from his brain. One that played over and over and wouldn't go away.

Willow showed up on Saturday morning without warning because she didn't have Kane's phone number and naturally Mr. Macho Security Man wasn't listed. She'd even Googled him and had come up with nothing. It was as if he didn't exist.

But she knew he was real. Elusive and possibly dangerous to her emotional well-being but real. He was an interesting combination of contrasts. A tough man who knew how to be tender. A rich man who chose to live simply.

She'd told herself to forget him, but that wasn't happening anytime soon. All she had to do was close her eyes to remember how she'd felt when he touched her. Last night she'd even dreamed about him.

So she braced herself for possible rejection, grabbed the tote bag on the passenger seat and climbed out of her car. She was halfway up the walk when the front door to the gatehouse opened.

He wore jeans and a long-sleeved shirt and looked sexy enough to melt chocolate.

"You came back," he said, his voice, not to mention his expression, giving nothing away.

"I'm here to see the cats, not you," she said with a smile, hoping he wouldn't guess that was a big, fat lie. "You don't have to panic."

"I don't panic."

Her smile widened. "I can think of a few girly conversations that would make you sweat. Want to test my theory?"

One corner of his mouth twitched. "Not especially."

"I didn't think so." She held her tote in both hands. "I would have called first, but you didn't give me your number. And don't bother telling me you didn't give it to me on purpose. I already know that. You were afraid I'd turn into stalker girl."

"I'm not afraid of you."

She walked toward him and braced herself for the impact of seeing those dark eyes and that mouth up close.

"You could be, and you know it," she said cheerfully. "Now let me inside."

She was operating mostly on bravado, but either he didn't know that or he was just going with it. He stepped aside to let her in.

She walked into the living room and was assaulted by memories. There was the chair where he'd carried her when she'd first hurt her ankle and that was the doorway to the hall that led to the bedroom.

Her skin heated as she remembered him touching her. She swung to face him, prepared to mention how it had been, but the words died unspoken.

His expression was one of polite interest—nothing more. There was no humor, no flash of fire, no *need*. It was as if it had never been.

He hadn't been kidding about the one night, she thought

sadly. If she were someone else, she might have tried tempting him, but hey, this was her. What was the point? Instead she would have to be happy for what they'd had and remind herself that at least he'd wanted her once.

She dropped her tote on the ottoman and crossed to the box by the fireplace. The mother cat was curled up with her three kittens. She purred as Willow approached.

"Hi, sweetie," Willow murmured. "How have you been? Your babies are bigger. Look at how big they're getting. Are you doing all right?"

The cat rubbed her head against Willow's hand. "Is she still eating well?" she asked.

"About twice what I think she should," he told her. "Stuff comes out the other end really regularly, too."

She smiled. "At least we know she's healthy. That's something. Have you thought of a name?"

"I'm not naming the damn cat."

"But you have to. She needs an identity."

"She's a stray."

Willow sat on the carpet and looked up at him. She had to tilt her head back until she could meet his gaze. "Everyone deserves to have a name."

His mouth tightened. "Fine. You name her."

"Okay." She looked back at the gray and white cat. "How about Muffin."

"Not Muffin."

"Why not?"

"It's a food. You don't name a cat after something you eat."

So he had opinions, she thought as she held in a smile. "Then Pookey."

Kane made a strangled sound. "No."

"You've made it very clear this isn't your cat. Why do you get veto power?"

"It's living in my house. I'll have to call it by the name. Not Pookey."

He could barely say the word. Willow ducked her head so he wouldn't see her grinning.

"Jasmine? Snowflake? Princess Leia?"

"Princess Leia?"

"I'm a *Star Wars* fan. More the first three than the last three, but I like them all."

"Good to know. I can live with Jasmine."

"Not Snowflake?"

"She's not white."

"Snow can be gray."

He made a sound that was more strangled groan than growl, but she couldn't be totally sure about that.

"Then Jasmine," she said as she stood. "Hi, Jasmine. Welcome to the family." And before Kane could point out they weren't a family, she grabbed her tote and headed for the kitchen. "I'm going to make cookies."

He followed her. "Here? In my kitchen?"

"In your oven, actually," she said as she set the temperature. "My powers of cooking through psychic energy aren't what they used to be."

"What if I don't want cookies?"

She looked at him. "Everyone wants cookies. They're chocolate chip. What's not to like?"

She pulled a baking pan out of her tote along with a package of premade cookie dough. All she had to do was break off the little squares, put them on the pan and stick them in the oven. Nearly instant fresh-baked cookies.

When the pan was ready, she leaned against the counter and looked at him. He looked good…too good. He made her wish things could be different, that he was secretly desperate to have her again. If only there was a scrap of evidence, she would cling to that fantasy, but so far…not so much.

She also knew that he could throw her out in a heart-beat, if that was what he really wanted. The cookies wouldn't matter to him. But as he made no move to bodily remove her, she settled in for a little visit.

"So," she said, "how are things?"

"It's not going to work," he told her.

"What isn't?"

"You're not going to convince me to get involved with you."

"I kind of know that. The cookies are just my way of being nice." And maybe hanging around for a little longer, which made her pathetic, but she could live with that.

His dark gaze settled on her face. She felt the weight of his attention down to her toes, which chose that moment to curl ever so slightly.

He was as big as she remembered. Big and powerful and totally masculine. Kane was not the kind of guy to get in touch with his feminine side. He was more likely to get a knife and cut it away.

"Why did you do it?" he asked. "Why did you sleep with me? I made the rules very clear and you're not that kind of woman."

She sighed. "Slutty, you mean? I know. I've never done that before. I mean sex, sure. A couple of times. But meeting a guy and jumping into bed with him…not ever. I think it was the blood loss. My brain wasn't working right."

That earned her a smile, which, unfortunately, faded quickly. "You weren't slutty. I still want to know why you did it."

"Do I confuse you?" she asked, hoping that was it because confusing and intriguing weren't all that different.

"A little. I know there's more going on than I can see."

Yeah!

He waited expectantly. She shifted, then folded her arms across her chest.

"It's kind of embarrassing," she said.

"I won't laugh."

She drew in a deep breath. He'd been honest about what he wanted and didn't want, so maybe she should be honest about why she'd done it...

"You wanted me," she said simply. "I liked you and trusted you. Being with you made me feel safe, but what pushed me over the edge was how much you wanted me."

He frowned. "You're available to any guy who's interested?"

She laughed. "No. Well, probably not. I don't know. Guys don't want me."

"You've said that before and it's crap. Of course they do. Look in the mirror. You're beautiful and funny. A little strange, but not psycho."

Compliments? Compliments before he'd even had cookies? She wanted to bask in the moment, but he looked impatient.

"I'm the best friend," she said. "I'm the one guys confide in, the one they tell their troubles to. I fix them and they go out and fall in love with someone else. I couldn't figure out what was wrong, then a couple of years ago I was at a party. I heard a group of guys talking. They were pretty drunk and going on about which of the girls at the party they'd like to sleep with. When they got to me, they all said they liked me, thought I was sweet, but I wasn't the kind of girl they wanted to...you know."

That was the easy part. She looked out the window over the sink and steeled herself to tell the rest. "I'd gone out with one of the guys and we'd…been together. He'd kind of been my first. I thought we were in love, but then he broke up with me and never really said why. That night he said he'd slept with me because he'd owed me. He'd been doing me a favor."

It still hurt. Not in the bone-crushing way it had at first, but enough to make her catch her breath.

"The second guy I was with said all the right things, but after the first time, he was never very interested in sex. He said it was me, that he'd never had any problems with other women."

"It wasn't you," Kane said flatly.

"You don't know that."

"Willow, I've seen you naked. I've touched you every-where possible. I've kissed you and tasted you and watched you come apart in my arms. It wasn't you."

Her eyes widened. He was good. Better than good. She felt her battered ego heal a little.

"But those guys, the things they said…"

Kane shook his head. "You're complicated. Guys, es-pecially young guys, want things simple. You scare them off. Or you take care of them so much they think you're their mother. But there's nothing wrong with you."

"But…"

He cut her off with a look. "Did I fake it?"

She smiled. "No. You were very clear about what you wanted."

"What did I want?"

"Me?" The single word came out in a squeak.

"You. Now let it go. You're fine."

Just then the oven dinged. She put in the pan of cookies and set the timer.

If only he wanted her again, she thought. But he'd been

clear about that, too. One night. She decided not to push her luck and instead changed the subject.

"How's Todd?" she asked.

"Why do you want to know?"

"Just making conversation. Does he know I was here?"

"I told him."

She laughed. "Was he scared?"

"No."

"Couldn't you have told him I was really scary?"

"No."

"Typical. I think he's safe. Julie and Ryan are so happy together, and he wasn't able to break them up, so I'm losing energy about the whole telling him off thing."

"Any plans to date him?" Kane asked.

"What?"

"I know about the million-dollar offer on the table."

Ah, yes. It was more than a fortune, she thought. "My grandmother is an interesting woman. I don't know why she made that ridiculous statement, but now we all have to deal with it. I'm not interested in marrying someone for money."

"It's a lot of money."

"I believe in falling in love. That my soul mate is my destiny. Money doesn't matter."

He shook his head. "Money always matters."

"That's cynical and sad."

"That's realistic."

"You've never been married, have you?"

"I don't do relationships, remember?"

Which was more than sad, she thought. It was tragic. "You have to connect to someone."

"Why?"

"It's how people are. We are the sum of our experiences,

our relationships. You can't tell me you're totally happy living on your own."

"I am, but you won't believe me."

"Kane, be serious. Don't you ever want more?"

He stunned her by walking toward her and crowding her back against the counter. He was close enough for her to feel the heat of his body. Close enough for her to see the various shades of brown and gold that made up the color of his eyes. Close enough for her to begin to melt with longing.

"This isn't going to work," he said in a low voice. "You can prance around all you want, but it's not going to change anything."

"Prance? I don't prance."

"You move, you sway, you glide, you intrigue. But I will not be tempted. This is over. We do not have nor will we ever have a relationship. It was a great night. Maybe the best night. If I were ever to reconsider my position, you'd be the one I'd do it for. But it's not going to happen. I will not let you in."

She opened her mouth, then closed it. He still wanted her. She could see the fire back in his eyes. Desire was there, but so was determination. She was thrilled and confused.

"Why not?" she asked. "What's so scary about a relationship?"

"I don't trust anyone," he said flatly. "I learned early that everyone was in it for himself. The only person I can depend on is me."

He was wrong—so wrong. But she didn't know how to convince him otherwise.

"What happened to you?" Had his parents abused him? Had a friend died?

His dark gaze locked with hers and she had a feeling she wasn't going to like what he had to say.

"I lived on the streets when I was a kid. Just me. I joined a gang to stay alive and they became my family. When I was sixteen, my girlfriend fell for a guy in a rival gang. She kept the relationship a secret. To prove her loyalty, she set me up. I was shot three times and left for dead by the only person I'd ever loved."

"What do you mean dead?" Marina asked as she passed the basket of rolls.

Willow took one and offered the rest to Julie who shook her head. "Her boyfriend shot Kane and drove off. Someone called for an ambulance and somehow he survived." Willow still couldn't believe that had happened, but she'd seen those scars on his body.

The sisters had met for lunch near Julie's office. It was one of those warm fall days that makes people in snow country think about moving to Los Angeles.

"I know what you're thinking," Marina told her. "That you can save him."

"Don't go there," Julie added. "He's not like the guys you usually rescue. He's dangerous."

Which made him even more appealing, Willow thought humorously. "He's alone. I think he needs someone in his life."

Marina looked at Julie then shook her head. "Let me guess. You're volunteering. Willow, sometimes guys mean what they say. He's not looking for any kind of relationship. You can't change him."

"But if he could just let himself risk it, he would be so much better off," Willow said.

Julie touched her arm. "You know I love you and I'll be there for you, no matter what, but why do you do this to yourself? You're always setting yourself up."

"It's just who I am," Willow said. "I want things to be different. I want a guy to love me and want to be with me forever. Maybe Kane's that guy."

"Maybe he's going to trample all over your heart," Julie said gently. "I hate to see you hurt again."

"I know."

Willow had possibly the worst luck in men. She fell for guys who weren't attracted to her. She saved them, healed them and they moved on to someone else.

"This is different," she said.

"Is it?" Julie asked. "How? No, wait. Don't answer that. Have you ever considered that you get involved with men you can never have so you don't have to risk falling in love? You say you want happily-ever-after, but you seem to go out of your way to make sure it never happens."

Willow looked from her to Marina. "I don't do that."

Marina sighed. "I'd have to agree with Julie on this one. You avoid normal men. Men who want to get married and have kids."

Willow opened her mouth, then closed it. She wanted to tell them both that they were wrong. She wasn't like that—except maybe she was.

Suddenly she was seventeen again, standing in her bedroom, getting ready for a date. She was fussing with her hair when her father walked in. He wasn't around much, so having him home was a big deal. She remembered putting down her brush and spinning in a circle.

"What do you think, Daddy? Am I pretty enough?"

Her father had looked at her for a long time. "You'll never be as smart and pretty as your sisters, but I'm sure you'll find someone to take care of you. Just don't aim too high, kid."

His words had cut through to her soul. She'd gone on

the date, but she remembered nothing about the night. Her father's words had burned themselves in her brain and left her gasping with pain.

She'd known that Marina and Julie were more beautiful and that she had to work harder in school to get lesser grades, but she'd never thought that mattered. Until that moment, she'd always believed she was special.

But if her own father didn't think so, maybe she wasn't. She'd never felt special again…until that night in Kane's arms.

"Willow?" Marina leaned toward her. "Are you okay?"

"I'm fine." She took a deep breath as the truth settled in her brain. "You're right. Both of you. I avoid regular guys because I'm afraid to take a chance on falling in love for real and being rejected. What was I thinking? I can't fix Kane. He doesn't want to have anything to do with me and I'm going to let him go. It's the right thing to do."

Julie bit her lower lip. "Are you all right? I didn't mean to hurt your feelings."

"You didn't. You're looking out for me and that's good."

"I love you," Julie said sincerely.

"Me, too," Marina added.

Willow felt their affection and it eased the hurt inside. Whatever else happened, she could count on her sisters to be there for her. As for Kane…she was going to let him go. He didn't want her around. The man couldn't have been more clear in his meaning.

Maybe it was time to stop chasing after the moon and settle here on earth where she belonged. Find a normal guy. So what, exactly, did normal look like?

Five

Kane walked into his house and heard the kittens crying. Usually they were silent, contentedly sleeping or nursing or being groomed by their mother. He dropped his briefcase onto a kitchen chair and moved into the living room where he found the kittens in their box, but no mother cat.

He quickly searched the house and there was no sign of her. But the window he'd left open for fresh air had been pushed open wider and the screen lay on the ground below. The mother cat was gone.

He swore under his breath and looked at the mewing kittens in the box. Now what? Was the mother cat gone for good? Had she abandoned her family? He did not need this crap in his life, he thought as he grabbed the phone, then realized he didn't have the number.

Three minutes later, he was dialing. His security

programs meant, with his trusty computer and decent Internet access, he could find anyone anywhere.

"Hello?"

He frowned. The voice wasn't familiar. "Willow?"

There was a sniff, followed by a shaky, "Yes."

Something was wrong. He didn't actually want to know what right now but knew it was polite to ask. Screw it, he thought a second later. "It's Kane."

She made a noise that sounded a lot like a sob. "What's wrong?" she asked, her voice thick with what he had a bad feeling was tears. "You wouldn't be calling if there wasn't something wrong."

She told the truth and he was good with that. So why did he feel a flash of guilt from her words?

"The cat is gone."

"Jasmine?"

Who the hell was… Oh, yeah. She'd named the cat. "Yes, Jasmine. I left a window open to get some air in this place. She managed to push out the screen and escape. The kittens are crying and I don't know what to do."

"Not leaving the window open would be a start," she said quietly. "I'll be right over."

Willow did her best to get control. She was not a pretty crier. There were no delicate tears rolling down a perfectly pale cheek. Instead she got blotchy, her eyes swelled and her nose wouldn't stop running. But even more importantly, she didn't want Kane to think she was crying over him. She wasn't. Her current pothole in the road of life had nothing to do with him. But men had such big egos. He would assume he'd crushed her.

She parked her car and used the last of her tissue to wipe her face. Then she blew her nose and drew in a breath. She ignored how she looked. What was important was finding Jasmine.

She stepped out of the car, prepared to call for the cat, but before she could say a word, Jasmine came strolling out of the bushes and meowed.

Willow crouched down and patted her. "Did you just need some alone time?" she asked. "Were the kids getting to you?"

Jasmine meowed again and rubbed against her fingers. The front door opened.

Willow straightened and braced herself for the impact of seeing Kane again. The man still looked good and her entire body sighed in appreciation. He was big and strong and looked as if he could take on the world.

Was it just a size thing, she wondered. If she were taller, would she be able to take on the world? Not that she was interested in all of it. But some control over her little corner would be nice.

"She's back," she said, pointing at Jasmine. "I think she just wanted to get out for a while. Did you try opening the door and calling for her?"

"Ah, no. I didn't think of that. I'm not a pet person."

"Obviously."

Kane stared from her to the cat and back. He shifted on his feet. If she didn't know better, she would think he felt a little foolish.

Maybe it was wrong, but that made her feel better. "I would suggest you check to make sure your screens are secure. Also, it wouldn't be a bad idea to let her out every morning, just so she can be on her own for a while. I'm sure it's draining to look after three babies all at once."

"Okay. Thanks. I will."

He stared at her. She had no idea what he was thinking and, at that moment, she didn't much care. She hurt from the inside out and it wasn't a pain that any pill could help. She'd been rejected in such a fundamental way. The worst part was, she hadn't been prepared. The news had come from nowhere.

"You want to come in?" he asked.

"Are there any cookies left?"

He nodded.

"Okay." Maybe chocolate would help.

She walked into the house. Jasmine came with her and gracefully jumped into the box with her kittens. They mewed frantically, until she licked each of them and they got quiet. Everything was all right in their world now, Willow thought, envious of their simple needs. Maybe she should have been a cat instead of a person. It looked like a better life.

"Have a seat," Kane said, motioning to the sofa.

Willow perched on a cushion. How strange to be back here. She'd already decided she would never see him again and here she was. While she could appreciate the thrill of watching his powerful body move through the room, she couldn't help thinking this was another place she'd been rejected. When she got home she would have to check her charts and see if Mercury was in retrograde.

Kane returned with a plate of her cookies and a bottle of water.

Despite the knot in her chest, she looked up at him and smiled. "Cookies and water? You know how to treat a girl right."

"Sorry. I don't have anything else to drink."

"It's fine."

As she spoke, a single tear ran down her cheek. That would have been okay, but she could feel others building up inside. She swallowed.

"Could you, um, get me some tissues?"

"Sure."

He bolted from the room. At any other time, his panic would have been amusing. Now she couldn't seem to find humor in anything.

When he returned with a box of tissues, she grabbed a couple and blotted her face.

"You don't have to get your panties in a twist," she said before blowing her nose. "This isn't about you."

"My panties?"

"You know what I mean. I'm not crying over you. I lost my syndication deal." Just saying it out loud made her start to cry again. "There'd been no warning. I thought things were going great. Then I got a call that they were dropping me. Too many people wrote in and said the comic strip wasn't funny or that they didn't get it."

She sucked in a breath and looked at him. He still hovered in front of the sofa, as if not sure where he should go.

"There were three girl squash. They were friends and dated and shopped. It was a lot like *Sex and the City*, only without the sex...or the city part, either. My girls lived on a farm. But not a real one. There was a mall and restaurants. They dated other vegetables. It was funny."

She ducked her head as more tears spilled down her cheeks. "How could people not get it? I worked so hard, too." That's what killed her. How she'd poured so much of herself into the comic strip.

"Are there other places you could sell it?" Kane asked.

"I don't think so. I was mostly in vegetarian magazines and newspapers. You know, the weekly kind. A few organic-focused newsletters picked me up, too. The girls were really into the organic, holistic lifestyle. They were very spiritual."

"The squash?"

She nodded. "It wasn't a lot of money, you know. I wasn't in a big magazine, but still. The money from that and the candle sales was enough for me to get by."

"You sell candles?"

"Uh-huh." She choked down a sob. "I know I'm not like my sisters, but I thought my life was really good. Small, but good. I had my candles and the girls. But now they're gone and I don't know what I'm going to do. Plus, they just called and said it wasn't funny and people didn't get it. Goodbye. Just like that. Not that they were sorry or that they knew how hard I worked. Do you know how many hours I spent on it each week? A lot."

Kane sat on the sofa and looked at her. "I'm sorry."

"Thanks. It's not you. It's just everything right now. I had lunch with my sisters a couple of days ago. They said I avoid normal men because I'm afraid to have a real relationship and I think they might be right. So I'm not just a failure, I'm emotionally stunted, too."

"You're not a failure. You had a setback."

That nearly made her laugh. "A setback? I have a crushed and broken career. Do you know my sister Julie passed the bar exam the first time? She works for a very high-powered international law firm and she's on the partner track. Marina, my younger sister, is so smart, she graduated from high school when she was fifteen and went to UCLA on a full scholarship. She got three different degrees in chemistry and physics. I don't even know exactly what they are. I think one is in inorganic chemistry, but I don't even know what that is. How lame is that? She has all kinds of grad schools begging her to attend. I mean begging. They came to the house and everything. Do you know what she's doing now?"

She looked at him. He was a little blurry around the edges, which was probably just her tears. "Do you?"

He shook his head.

"She's taken a couple of years off of school and she's working as a sign language interpreter for the deaf. She specializes in all those science classes she studied. She's giving back. Being a good person. I can't even sell a cartoon about squash. They're both so smart and pretty and I don't fit in with them anymore."

Kane felt as if he'd descended into the seventh level of hell. Willow's obvious pain made him uncomfortable and he had no idea what to say to her. The only thing that came to mind was a feeble, "You're pretty."

"Oh, please. You said I was scrawny." She blew her nose and reached for another tissue.

He swore silently. "You were right," he told her. "It was the sweater. You have great..." He raised his hands and lowered them. "You're very sexy. I wanted you, remember?"

She turned to him, her face swollen and blotchy, her eyes red. "Wanted. In the past tense. For a single night. You said that's all it would be and you were right. So I'm good enough for one night, but not to tempt you again."

Couldn't she have just shot him? That would have been easier and less painful, he thought grimly. It was like being trapped in quicksand. The more he struggled, the deeper he sank.

"Don't worry," she said. "I don't want you now. I'm not interested in mercy sex."

"I... You..."

She drew in a shaky breath, then more tears poured down her cheeks. "Dammit, Kane, you could have made a pass at me just now, so I could have turned you down. It's the polite thing to do."

Then she really began to cry, with body-shaking sobs and harsh breaths. He wasn't just in a foreign country—

he'd fallen into a different galaxy. He didn't know how to handle this or her. There were probably words that would make her feel better, but nothing in his experience had taught him what they were.

Women passed through his life without ever touching him. He knew their bodies and their heat, but nothing about their souls or hearts. Willow had been hurt on a fundamental level. While he could understand that, he didn't know how to fix it.

Slowly, feeling both awkward and stupid, he put his arm around her. She turned into him, leaning against his chest, her face pressing into his shoulder. He held her more tightly, feeling the small bones of her back. She was so fragile, he thought. He could crush her without breaking a sweat. Yet in other ways, she was strong and powerful.

Her tears dampened his shirt. He held her close, rubbing up and down her back. He should probably say something, but had no clue as to what, so he stayed silent. Eventually the tears slowed and she drew in a deep breath.

"I'm going to have a fight with my sister," she said quietly.

"Because it's on your calendar for this week?"

He couldn't see her face so he didn't know if she'd smiled, but he hoped she had.

"Because my dad is coming home. Mom called and told me last night. Julie always gets angry and critical when he shows up. He's not like other fathers. He doesn't stick around for long. My mom's okay with that. They're in love, or at least she loves him and she says what she has is enough. I believe her, but Julie doesn't. She says Mom needs more than a husband who visits once or twice a year, stays for a few months, then disappears."

"Where does he go?"

"I don't know. None of us do. It's just what he's always done. The thing is Marina can totally accept him and Julie will never forgive him. They're definitive. People should be definitive."

He ran his fingers through her long blond hair. The cool strands were silky soft and damned erotic. "Why?"

This time she chuckled. "Because it provides order. I'm the middle child, cursed with the ability to see all sides of things. It's annoying for me and those around me."

He touched her chin, forcing her to look at him. Her eyes were the color of the Caribbean Sea. Even puffy, she was beautiful. Her full mouth called to him. Desire flared and he suddenly wanted her with an intensity that hit him like a gunshot.

"Kane? Are you all right?"

"I'm fine."

Shaken, but fine.

What was wrong with him? He'd had her for a night— that was enough. It was always enough. He needed to distract them both.

"Did you like drawing the cartoons?" he asked.

Instantly her eyes clouded. "Of course. It was fun and creative. Sometimes I didn't like the pressure of the deadline. It was very much an every week thing. I was usually late, which isn't good."

"Was it your dream? Did you grow up wanting to be a cartoonist?"

Her eyes cleared as she smiled. "No. It was not my childhood fantasy."

"What was?"

She pulled back and wiped her face with her hand. "I'm sorry to break down like this. You only wanted help with your cat and I've gotten your shirt wet."

She placed her fingertips on the damp fabric. Her touch burned him down to the bone.

He ignored the need and instead focused on the woman. "You didn't answer the question."

"I know. I just…it's so small, you know? Julie's doing big things and Marina's going to save lives or maybe the planet. I'm not like that."

"Why do you have to be?"

"I don't, but if I'm not, do I still belong?"

Her pain made him uncomfortable. He wanted to fix the problem, which he couldn't. He barely understood it. Women and their feelings were a mystery he'd never wanted to solve…until today.

"You'll always be a part of your family," he told her. "Maybe if you were doing what you wanted to do instead of what you thought you should, you wouldn't care about being different."

She blinked at him. "That's good. Do you read self-help books?"

He grimaced. "No."

"I didn't think so. You're not the type. I want…" She drew in a breath and said, "I love plants. I love how they're all so different. I love making them grow, especially the really tough ones. I love how they look and feel and smell and how they all have different personalities."

Personalities? Plants? He told himself to just go with it. This was Willow, after all.

"Sometimes, when they change overnight, it's like magic," she said. "I want to open a nursery."

She paused, then seemed to fold in on herself, as if waiting for an attack. "Dumb, huh?"

"It's not dumb," he told her. "Why couldn't you?"

"I don't know anything about business. I didn't go to

college, I've never even worked in a nursery. It takes money to start a business."

"You could marry Todd. A million dollars is a lot of start-up capital."

That earned him a big smile. "Very funny."

She leaned back against the sofa, which trapped his arm behind her neck, but he wasn't inclined to pull it back.

"Okay, I'll be serious. You get a job in a nursery and learn the business. You go to community college and take business classes."

She turned to look at him. "You make it sound simple."

"Why does it have to be hard? When I was in the hospital and the army recruiter stopped in to see me, I realized it was a way out. I couldn't stay where I was— they'd only come after me again. I already had a fake birth certificate saying I was eighteen, so when I was released, I joined up. If it's important, you do what you have to do. It doesn't have to be hard. Willow, you got me to adopt a damn cat. Trust me, you can make a business work."

"You think?"

"I know."

She smiled then, a warm, welcoming happy smile that made him want to strip her naked and take her in ways she didn't know existed.

Instead he leaned forward and handed her a cookie.

Later, when Willow had left and he was alone with the cat, Kane glanced at the feline who seemed to be watching him with great interest.

"Don't get any ideas," he told her. "I only called Willow because you needed your own space. It won't happen again. I don't like her. I don't like anyone, including you."

The cat blinked slowly.

"Just as soon as your kittens are older, I'm taking all of you to the pound. Just so you're clear."

The cat blinked again and the sound of her purring filled the quiet room.

Six

Willow sorted through the beads on the table in front of her, chose one and picked up her glue gun. She carefully applied the bead to one of the candles she'd finished the previous night and did her best not to grin as Kane paced the length of her small kitchen.

It took him all of three steps before he had to turn around and go the other way. She'd offered him a seat, but he seemed determined to stand during their conversation.

She wouldn't have minded if he didn't look so...uncomfortable. Probably her place, she thought as she glanced around. It was pretty girly—all ruffles and ribbons on the curtains she'd made. There were plants everywhere, along with candles and dishes of potpourri. She had a small collection of china and crystal unicorns on a shelf in the living room. Her furniture there was white wicker with floral cushions.

Definitely not Kane's kind of place.

"I'll be gone two nights," he said as he glanced at a pot holder in the shape of a frog and grimaced. "I'm sure the cat will be fine, but if you could feed her—"

"I'm happy to," Willow told him, holding in her smile. "I'll put out fresh food, change the litter, give her a little attention." She paused and prepared to enjoy the moment. "This means you'll be giving me a key."

"Yes."

"To your house."

"I know."

She picked up another bead. "It will be like we're living together."

He turned and stared at her. "We're not living together."

"I didn't say we were."

"You implied it. You're looking after the cat, that's it. The cat you insisted I keep. I shouldn't have the cat at all."

"But you do."

His mouth thinned. "You're to take care of her and then leave. Don't go through my stuff."

She pretended to be insulted. "Would I do that? Honestly, Kane, when have I violated your personal space?"

"You want a list? I know you," he growled. "You'll snoop."

This was so much fun, she thought happily. He was just adorable when he was grumpy. "I promise I won't."

"As if I believe that."

"Hey, I don't lie. I won't look around."

"I'll know if you do."

He probably would. So what would he do? Put single hairs across drawers and sticky spy stuff on the inside of closets?

"I gave my word," she told him. "I meant it. Take whatever precautions make you happy, but there's no need. I'll respect your privacy."

He eyed her for a second, then put a key on the counter.

She sighed. "This is so sudden. I thought you wanted to take things more slowly."

He gaze narrowed.

She grinned. "I can't help it. You're just so easy."

"Thanks."

She turned off the glue gun, then stood. "I don't mean that in bad way. You're just fun to bug."

"I'm ignoring you now."

"You can't. It's my apartment and I'm in charge. Besides, you'll be interested in this."

She walked into the living room and picked up a catalog from the glass and wicker coffee table. "Look," she said as she waved it. "This is for the spring semester at my local community college. I'm going to sign up for business classes. And I've been looking at getting a job in a nursery." She paused for effect. "I have an interview on Thursday."

His tortured expression relaxed. "Good for you."

"Thanks. I never thought about just taking the steps. I guess they didn't seem possible. But now they are and it's all thanks to you."

"I only pointed you in the right direction."

"You don't want to take credit?"

"No."

"But then I'd owe you."

He stiffened.

She grinned. "Am I bugging you? I don't mean to."

"Yes, you do."

"Okay, a little, but in the nicest way possible. Admit it, Kane. You've never known anyone like me and I'm growing on you."

"Like mold." He folded his arms across his chest. "I see you're feeling better. Back in power and sassy."

"Sassy." She liked the sound of that. It was fun and

sexy. Is that how he saw her? She felt a little zing shoot through her.

"Don't read too much into that," he grumbled.

"Of course not. You don't do relationships." She tilted her head as she looked at him. "What about friends? Any of them hanging around?"

"No."

"No significant other, no family, no friends." Her good mood faded. "That's about the saddest thing I've ever heard," she murmured. Was it really possible that he didn't love anyone—and no one loved him? Her heart began to ache.

"Don't go there," he told her.

"Where?"

"Wherever it is you're planning on going. I like my life."

"Don't you ever want more?"

"No."

He spoke flatly, as if trying to convince her, but she refused to believe him. What happened in the dark of night when he was alone? Didn't he want a friend to share things with? Someone to care? To miss him when he was gone and welcome him home again?

Without thinking, she crossed the few feet between them and hugged him. He pulled his arms free, but didn't touch her. She felt his stiffness, his resistance to the embrace.

"I don't need this, Willow."

"Maybe I do. Just accept it and hug me back."

For a long time, she thought he was going to ignore her or push her away. But at last, she felt his arms embrace her.

She stood holding him, breathing in his tempting, masculine scent, feeling his heat and his strength. He was the most dangerous man she'd ever known, yet she couldn't be afraid of him. He still made her feel safe.

Crazy talk, she told herself. She should ignore it. Except she felt a strong and deep connection to Kane. It was as if some part of him called to her.

Was that real or just her burning desire to rescue the world? Not that he would believe he needed rescuing.

She looked up and met his gaze. The sexual fire there stole her breath away. Wanting swept through her as she imagined being with him again. She became aware of all the places her body touched his and how much better that touching would be if they were both naked.

"You want me," she breathed.

He immediately stepped back. "It doesn't matter."

Was he kidding? "Of course it matters. It's fabulous. Let's go do it."

She grabbed his hand and tried to pull him toward the bedroom, but he didn't budge. She spun back to face him.

"What on earth is wrong with you?" she demanded.

"I have rules for a reason."

"You're stubborn and difficult and your rules are stupid."

"That's only your opinion," he told her.

"But you *want* me," she said. "You totally want me."

"Yes, I do. And I'm not going to do anything about it."

"Kane?" She was trying not to take this personally, but it was hard.

He walked to the door. "I'll be back on Thursday in the early evening."

He was leaving? Just like that? Nothing he did made sense to her. Didn't any of this matter? Didn't *she* matter?

But she wasn't going to ask that last question—her ego was still a little bruised from the cancellation of the syndication deal. Better to not go there until she was stronger.

"You probably don't want me waiting for you," she said.

"You're right."

He was so solitary—it wasn't good. "Don't you ever want to come home to someone? To a bright house and a hot meal and a person who's happy to see you?"

Something flashed through his eyes. She couldn't tell what it was, but if pressed, she would have said a combination of pain and longing.

"I'm not interested in any of that," he said and then he was gone.

Willow stared after him. She might not know anything about being a lawyer or chemistry or even how to run a business, but she did know one thing.

Kane had been lying.

Thursday afternoon Willow pulled up in front of her apartment. She couldn't stop grinning, which was a good thing. Her interview had been amazing. She and Beverly, the owner of the nursery, had talked about plants and gardening and their favorite ways of doing things for nearly two hours. At the end, Beverly had not only offered her the job, but had upped the starting salary by two dollars an hour, with a promise of more money to come.

"You're exactly who I've been looking for," Beverly had told her. "I never thought I'd find you."

Words to make her do the happy dance, Willow thought as she climbed out of her car and walked toward her front door.

But her good mood evaporated like mist in the sun when she saw a familiar motorcycle parked against the side of her building and saw a tall, lanky man standing nearby.

Chuck was back.

Funny how in the past those three little words had always made her heart beat faster and her spirit wonder if this time he finally wanted to stick around. Because Chuck was an unfortunate combination of a man who needed rescuing—like nearly all the other men in her life—and her father—a man who couldn't stay in one place more than a few months.

The combination made him a poor bet for a romantic relationship and therefore nearly irresistible to her.

"Willow," he said as she approached. "It's been a long time. You look great."

"Chuck."

She looked at him, at the familiar too-long dark hair, the catlike green eyes, the sexy smile and braced herself for the emotional meltdown. Only there wasn't one. She felt exactly…nothing.

Willow came to a stop on the sidewalk. Wait a minute. This was Chuck—the one guy she most wanted to be with. The one she'd dreamed about, fantasized about, the one she'd wanted to have kids with.

"You changed your locks," he said, motioning to the door. "I couldn't get inside."

"Yes, I did change them." About six months ago, in a fit of self-preservation.

"Aren't you going to invite me in?"

She didn't have all that much to say to him, but why not? If this new attitude continued, she could consider herself cured.

"Sure."

She opened the door and led him inside. He looked around and grinned.

"Just like I remember," he said. "You've done it up so pretty."

Pretty? "You always said my place looked like a girls-only decorating catalog vomited on the place."

"Did I? I didn't mean it. You have great taste, Willow."

He moved close and put his arm around her. "You're looking good. Sexy."

Sexy? Wait a minute. "Since when?" she demanded. "You said after that one time we did it you thought of me as your sister."

"Nah, that wasn't me. I think you're hot."

Hot? Her? It was the answer to all her prayers. She waited for the rush of relief, the bubble of happiness. Instead she found herself wondering what kind of dirt he was tracking in on her clean floor.

She slipped free of his embrace and moved into the kitchen where she poured two glasses of iced tea.

"I did it, Willow," he said as he leaned against the counter. "I cleaned up my life, the way you always told me to. I moved to Tucson and got a job and saved my money. Whenever I wanted to do something stupid, I'd ask myself, 'Would Willow do this?' and then I'd listen to the answer. I won a bunch of money playing poker and I bought me a Jiffy Lube franchise. They're a great company and I'm doing good. I'm saving for a house, too."

She didn't know what to think. It was too much information all at once.

"Good for you," she said and meant it. She was glad he'd found what he wanted.

"The thing is, I don't want to go back to the way I was," he told her, sounding painfully earnest. "I need you in my life, Willow. I'm a better man with you around. So I was thinking, you could come back with me. We'd live together for a while and if that went as good as I think it's going to, we'll get married. You want that, right? Marriage and some kids? I can give that to you now."

A year ago she would have been melting in a puddle of excitement. Having Chuck finally speak those words—although maybe not as romantically as she would have liked—would have meant everything to her. Now, she felt nothing.

What was wrong with her? Sure, she'd sworn off the whole rescuing thing, but this was Chuck. Shouldn't he have tested her resolve?

"I wish you the best," she said sincerely. "I'm so happy for you and proud of what you've done with your life, but I'm not interested in moving to Tucson."

He moved close and cupped her cheek. "Hey, Willow. It's me."

Then he lowered his head and kissed her.

She waited for the familiar rise of heat and longing, or at least a sense of revenge. After all, Chuck had slept with her and then told her he didn't find her appealing in that way.

She felt the warmth of his mouth and a hint of wanting in his kiss. And that was it. She didn't tingle or strain or even kiss him back. Honestly, what was the point?

He straightened. "What's wrong?"

"Nothing." Which was true, she thought happily. "Absolutely nothing."

"I'm saying I want you in my life," he told her. "You've been waiting for that."

"Apparently not as much as we both thought," she told him, trying not to smile. She felt light and free and totally at peace with herself.

"But…" he began.

She stepped back. "Chuck, I think it's terrific that you've found everything you want. I'm glad I had some small part in that. But you don't need me to be successful. Go find someone you can really love and settle down. That will make you happy."

"But you're the one I want," he said stubbornly.

"Not really. I'm an old habit. I've always rescued you, but here's the thing. I don't do that anymore, which is great, because you don't need rescuing. You're doing fine on your own."

He looked more confused than annoyed. "But I came back for you."

"Which was really sweet of you."

"You're supposed to be in love with me."

"Not anymore." Maybe never, she thought. It was a real possibility she'd mistaken her longing for a fantasy for the real thing.

He swore. "I should have come back sooner."

She hated to think that might have made a difference, but it could have. She shuddered to think she might have actually gone off with Chuck at one time. What a nightmare. However would she have found her way home?

She glanced at the clock on the wall. "I need to get going. I have to be somewhere."

He grabbed her arm. "Is it someone else? Is there another guy?"

If only, she thought, knowing she was completely cured of wanting men who didn't much want her. "No. It's a cat. I'm pet-sitting for a friend."

"If it's about the money," he said, "I'll pay you back."

And pigs would soon be flying across the west side of Los Angeles. "That would be great."

She removed his hand from her arm, then gently pushed him toward the front door. She grabbed her purse and keys on the way.

"Thanks for stopping by. It's been really great to see you, Chuck. I wish you every happiness."

Once they were safely outside, she locked the door behind her and made her way to her car.

"Good luck," she called back to him. "I mean that. I know the right woman is out there, waiting for you."

He didn't wave back or say anything. Willow drove off, made a few turns in the neighborhood, then, when she was sure Chuck was gone, returned to her place.

She ran inside and collected candles and more cookies she'd made. Kane might claim to be comfortable coming home to a dark and empty house, but she knew that wasn't true. She wanted to make him feel welcome. Plus, she was celebrating the fact that she'd been extra good. In all the times she'd gone over to take care of Jasmine and her babies, Willow had never once looked anywhere she shouldn't. She hadn't even flipped through his magazines. For all she knew, she was going to be crowned Miss Privacy Minder of the month.

She drove over to Kane's house and went inside. Jasmine greeted her with a little meow and lots of purring. Willow crouched down and petted her, then gently stroked the kittens. Two of them already had their eyes open.

"Hi, babies," she said softly. "You're getting so big. Yes, you are. Guess who comes home tonight? Kane. Are you excited? I'm excited."

After feeding Jasmine and cleaning out the litter, Willow returned to her car and began collecting her bags. She was on her way back when an unwelcome and familiar sound made her turn.

Chuck drove his motorcycle down the driveway and pulled up next to her. He took off his helmet and walked toward her.

"There's someone else," he said flatly. "You lied to me."

"I didn't lie. I told you I was cat-sitting. Want to see the cat?"

He grabbed one of the bags and opened it. "Candles and cookies. I know you, Willow. There's a guy."

"So what if there is? Why are you surprised? I've moved on with my life, Chuck. You've been gone for months and this isn't the first time you left. Did you think I'd wait forever?"

His stunned expression told her that the answer was yes. How pathetic...for both of them, she thought grimly.

"You always waited," he told her.

"Maybe before, but not anymore. I'm not that person you remember. Things are different for me."

"Who's the guy?"

"We're just friends."

"Like I believe that." He dropped the bag on the ground and stepped toward her. "Who's the guy?"

His face sharpened with anger. She'd never seen Chuck as someone with a temper. He'd always gone with the flow.

He raised his hand and for a second, she thought he was going to hit her.

Kane wove through traffic on his way home. He felt a pressing need to be at his house, which he didn't like. Why did he care where he was? But the desire was there, so he drove a little faster, while telling himself it didn't matter when he arrived. It wasn't as if Willow was going to be there.

Not that he wanted to see her. Or the damn cat. He would admit to some curiosity about the kittens. Maybe they'd grown a little since he'd been gone. Their eyes should be opening. That could be interesting.

He turned down a side street, then hit the remote control device that opened the large wrought-iron gate that led to his place. It was a shorter route than going down by the main house, and more private. He eased his Mercedes forward and checked to make sure the gate had closed behind him.

He rounded the corner and saw Willow standing in front of his place with some guy. It took Kane less than two seconds to read the fear in her body language and the intent in the man's raised hand.

He parked and got out of his car. His movements were deceptively slow, but inside, he felt tension build. The guy looked ready to take on someone and Kane was more than happy to oblige.

"Is this him?" the intruder asked Willow as Kane approached. "Is he the reason you won't come back with me?"

"I won't come back with you because I don't want to," she told him firmly. "I'm not interested in having a relationship with you, Chuck. Now go away."

Chuck laughed. "I don't think so."

Willow looked at Kane. "I'm sorry about this. Kane, this is Chuck. Somebody I used to know."

Chuck glared at her and swore. Although he'd lowered his hand to his side, he was still standing too close and doing his best to intimidate Willow. But she wasn't one to be pushed around. Kane saw her square her shoulders and stare right back at the jerk, as if to prove he couldn't scare her.

"Willow's mine," Chuck said, still glaring at Willow "I'm taking her with me."

Kane felt the slow burn build. He stood ready to attack, but without knowing if he should. He didn't mind being annoyed by this ass, what concerned him was the reason—Willow.

He shouldn't want to protect her, but he did. He shouldn't want to claim, yet the need to grab her and brand her with his mouth and his body grew with each passing second. He knew better than to feel anything, ever, yet the emotions would not be denied.

Kane walked toward Chuck. "Is there any part of you that thinks I'm going to let you take Willow anywhere?"

Chuck met his gaze and blinked first. "I, ah…"

"You could try it," Kane continued. "I think that would be fun. Come on. Try it."

Chuck paled and took a step back.

"You were so eager to force her," Kane said. "Were you going to hit her? It looked like you were. Are you the kind of girly man who gets his kicks from hitting women? Because where I'm from, that's lower than low. We use guys like you for wiping up the floor. That could be fun, too."

Chuck raised both hands in the air. "I didn't hurt her. Ask her, she'll tell you."

Kane continued to stare at him. "Get on your bike and get out of here. Never see Willow again. In fact, you should avoid L.A. altogether. Is that clear?"

Chuck nodded several times, then hurried to his bike. Seconds later, he was gone.

Kane stared after him. There was too much boiling inside of him. He should have fought the guy—it would have burned off energy.

He turned to Willow, who studied him. "You're never boring," he said. "I'll give you that."

She smiled. "Welcome home."

Seven

Kane led the way into the house. Willow followed him and closed the door.

"I don't know what happened," she said, both confused by Chuck's behavior and relieved that Kane had shown up when he had. "He's never been the least bit possessive. He was more the needy type and very into himself. Honestly, he's never been all that interested in me. And let me be clear. I didn't invite him here. He was waiting at my place earlier. We talked, I told him it was over and then I left. I guess he followed me. It's just so strange."

"It's not strange," Kane said, looking at her. "You were always available before. This time, you weren't. That made him want you more."

"Talk about twisted," she murmured, suddenly caught up in how good Kane looked. He wore a tailored suit that emphasized his muscles, not to mention the breadth of his shoulders. Now if he'd been the one asking her to run off to Tucson, she would have been gone in a flash.

"It's human nature. We want what we can't have."

Hmm, so was that why she wanted Kane? Because she couldn't have him?

Willow considered the question, then shook her head. No, she had a feeling she would be even more interested in Kane if he were begging her to stay. Not that he ever would. He was a pretty together guy. Now that she knew him better, she had to admit he didn't need much in the way of rescuing—except maybe emotionally and how likely was that to happen?

"He's going to have to get over it," she said firmly. "I'm done with the loser stage of my life. No more fixing guys up and sending them on their way. I'm my own person and I don't need to prove my worth by what I do for others."

He raised one eyebrow. "Read that in a magazine?"

"Uh-huh. Pretty cool. I was thinking of putting it on a pillow."

"Of course you were."

She grinned, then grabbed his hand and dragged him over to the window. Well, *drag* was kind of a strong word. She gave a tug, indicating where she wanted him to go and he did.

"Look," she said. "Flowers. Pretty."

"You're mocking me," he told her.

"Only a little. Okay, these little pots have herbs in them. Basil and rosemary, because of how they smell. I know you're not much for the cooking thing. Always keep rosemary in its own container, because it has designs on taking over the world. Then these two are flowers. Miniature roses. They're surprisingly easy to take care of and I love the colors."

"Okay."

She waited, hoping for more. She knew he wasn't excited about the plants, but could he accept them?

"What?" he asked.

"You could pretend to be interested."

"Would you believe me?"

"I'd try."

He sighed. "They're great. Thanks."

"You're welcome."

She tugged on his hand again. "Come see the kittens. Two of them have their eyes open."

He allowed her to lead him to the other side of the room. Jasmine meowed when she saw him, rose, stretched and jumped out of the box.

Kane bent down and petted her. Willow watched and wished he were petting her instead. Not that she wanted the underside of her chin scratched, but there were other lonely places.

"So how was your trip?" she asked when he'd straightened.

"Fine."

"Coffee?"

He hesitated, then said, "Sure."

Once they were in the kitchen, she poured in water and reached into the refrigerator for the bag of coffee.

"I was very good while you were gone," she said as she measured grounds. "I didn't look in anything. No drawers, no cupboards, nothing."

"Then how did you know where I keep my coffee?"

She smiled smugly. "I saw you get it when I was here before. On second thought, I wasn't good, I was perfect."

"How hard was it?"

She flipped on the coffeemaker. "Pretty hard, but I have

character and backbone. Plus, I gave my word and I try to respect that."

He stared down at her. She felt the intensity of his gaze all the way to her toes. Was there fire flickering there or was that wishful thinking on her part?

"How many other guys have there been?" he asked. "Guys like Chuck?"

Not the direction she wanted for this conversation. "A couple."

He continued to look at her.

"A few," she added. "Maybe more than a few."

"You try to fix them all?"

"Pretty much, but sometimes it works. Look at Chuck. He owns a Jiffy Lube. That's pretty impressive."

"I'm nearly faint with shock," Kane said dryly. "Are you still planning to rescue me?"

"You know, I was just thinking about that. The thing is, you don't really need rescuing. Your life is fairly together. Except for the whole alone thing. That's unfortunate."

"Maybe I like the silence."

"No one wants to be alone all the time. Admit it—you kind of liked having me here when you got home."

"Sure. Pulling up and seeing some guy prepared to slap you was great fun."

"Oh, yeah." She'd forgotten about that part. "I'm sure he didn't mean it."

"I'm sure he did." Kane moved closer. "You're a danger to yourself. You get involved and then you don't know how to get uninvolved. You need to work on that."

She felt the heat from his body. She supposed she could have been intimidated by him—after all he was looming. But this was Kane. He was strong and powerful, but she believed down to her bones all she had to do was say no and he would stop. He was so confident, he could afford to be gracious. Not that he would ever think of himself as gracious and he'd be annoyed to know she did.

"Are you going to fix me?" she asked, meeting his gaze and catching her breath at the fire she saw burning there. The glorious, hungry need was back.

"You're beyond fixing."

"You could try."

"I have other things in mind."

Yeah! She reached over and turned off the coffeepot. "Are you going to give me that speech again? The one about you never calling and how it's only for tonight and to have no expectations because you're only going to break my heart?"

He hesitated so long, she wanted to call the words back. She knew he was violating his rules and maybe pushing him would cause him to have second thoughts. Then he spoke.

"No."

Her heart jumped, her sides began that melting thing and she wanted to rip off her clothes right there in the kitchen.

"Really?" Her voice was a squeak.

"Really."

He leaned in, about to kiss her. She put her fingers on his mouth.

"Would you have beat up Chuck?"

"If he'd touched you."

"You mean if he'd hurt me?"

He gaze sharpened. "No. If he'd touched you."

Then he kissed her.

His mouth was hot and firm and soft and she wanted to give him everything. He wrapped his arms around her and drew her against him.

He was already hard and she squirmed to get closer, to feel all of him, especially his need.

He cupped her face in both hands, then deepened the kiss. His tongue swept inside her mouth, claiming her with an intensity that excited her.

"What is it about you?" he asked, his voice low and thick. "Why can't I get you out of my head?"

"I'm pretty irresistible," she said with a grin.

He raised his head and gazed into her eyes, but he wasn't smiling. "Yes, you are."

He bent down, gathered her in his arms and carried her toward the bedroom. Once there, he set her on her feet and put his hands on her shoulders.

"Tell me if you want this," he said.

He had to ask? How cute. "I want *you*, Kane."

He shuddered, then reached for her. She flung herself at him and when their bodies were pressed together from shoulder to knee, she felt as if she'd finally found her way home.

He touched her everywhere. His fingers explored her back, her hips, before lightly touching her arms. She both longed for the contact and wished he would touch her elsewhere—her breasts, between her legs, the places that ached.

Instead he drew her sweater over her head and leaned in to press his mouth to her shoulders. He licked and kissed and nipped, leaving goose bumps and tingles in his wake. He moved up her neck, along her jaw, then jumped to her earlobe where he bit down and sucked.

She had to cling to him to remain standing. Her legs trembled, her thighs nearly caught fire. Hunger consumed her, making her want to be reckless. She tugged at his tie and managed to loosen the knot, then she went to work on the buttons down the front of his shirt.

Her good intentions faded away when he placed his hands

on her breasts. He cupped her curves and used his thumbs to tease her tight, aching nipples. Her eyes sank closed as sensation washed through her. Oh, yeah, that was good.

Around and around, arousing her until she found it hard to keep breathing. Then he made it more difficult by kissing her.

While his tongue mated with hers, he dropped one hand to the waistband of her black slacks. Seconds later he'd unfastened the button and lowered the zipper. Then his fingers were between her thighs and all coherent thought fled her brain.

There was only the moment and man and the magic he created. The way he immediately found her most sensitive spot and began courting it. He circled and stroked, moving closer, then away. Teasing, exciting until she wanted to grab his wrist and force him to get to it.

But she didn't. The anticipation was too sweet.

He continued to touch her and kiss her. With his free hand, he reached behind her and opened her bra. One-handed—a great trick.

She lowered her arms so the scrap of lace could fall to the floor, then caught her breath as he ducked down and took her right nipple in his mouth.

Exquisite desire coiled through her, pulsing with each gentle suck of his lips. His tongue flicked against her tight tip, perfectly matching the arousing massage between her legs. She felt herself tensing, reaching, wanting.

"Kane," she breathed. "I can't hold back."

Which was, apparently, the wrong thing to say, because he stopped. Before she could protest, he'd taken off her shoes, her slacks, her socks and her panties. When she was naked, he made quick work of his own clothes, grabbed a condom, then led her to the bed.

After she'd stretched out on the bed, he knelt between her legs and pressed an openmouthed kiss against her center.

She remembered him doing this last time—how great he'd made her feel, the ease with which she'd found her release. Now she let herself relax into the sensations he drew out from her.

Need coiled deep within her, making her muscles tense, her body strain. She dug her heels into the bed and thrust herself toward him.

Closer and closer she spiraled. Up and up, with the soft stroke of his tongue driving her nearer to her goal. Waves of heat washed over her, the sound of her rapid breathing filled the quiet of the night.

"Almost," she gasped as he moved faster. "Almost."

And then she was there. Her body shuddered and quaked and she gave herself up to the pleasure. Over and over the contractions swept through her, making her moan and savor and smile. It was good—it was better than good. It was practically a miracle.

She opened her eyes and found him watching her. "You're really good at that," she murmured.

"I'm inspired."

While she'd been basking, he'd put on his condom. She reached between them and guided him inside, then sucked in a breath as she felt another little tingle. Talk about a great way to end the day.

She wrapped her legs around his hips and drew him in closer. He supported himself on his forearms and stared into her eyes as he filled her, then retreated. Over and over, still looking at her, exposing himself as he got closer.

Willow didn't break the contact. She saw the fire of his need and something else. Something dark and broken that called to her. His heart? His soul?

Her heart trembled at the idea of this lonely man sharing so much with her. Had anyone else ever seen inside?

She had no answer for the question, then even the questions were gone as the power of his body brought her once again to the brink. Her muscles tensed as she strained to reach her release.

Each thrust filled her, pushing her closer until she cried out and gave in. Involuntarily she closed her eyes, then he lost himself in her and they were still.

Kane sat in the living room, a drink in his hand. It was well after midnight and the house was still. Even the damn cat was asleep.

A single small lamp in the corner cast more shadows than light, but that suited his mood.

He'd broken his own rules. Rules he'd put in place after caring about someone…a woman…had nearly got him killed. Wasn't being shot in the gut and left for dead enough of a message? Why would he risk this again? Connecting, getting involved only made him weak. He had to stay strong—it was the only way to stay alive.

A logical argument, he thought. Except he couldn't be logical—not when he was talking about Willow.

He couldn't say why she was the one to get to him. Why her and not the one before or the one to come after? What combination of features and body language and scent and sound made him want to forget what he knew was right?

But it was her, and he didn't know how to escape the trap. She haunted him. Even when he was thousands of miles away, he'd remembered her.

He stared at the large package on the coffee table. With his business in New York complete and several hours before his flight, Kane had done something he'd never done before…gone shopping.

The act hadn't been conscious. He'd left his lunch meeting and started walking. But instead of heading for his hotel and then the airport, he'd gone north, toward the exclusive shops with their trendy window displays. He'd looked in them, ignoring clothes and jewelry, looking for what he wasn't sure. Until he'd found it.

A large tote bag covered in plants. It was bright and cheerful and ridiculously expensive, yet the second he'd seen it, he'd known it should be hers. He'd bought it and brought it home and now he was stuck with it.

He should send it back, he thought as he took another sip of his drink. He could pretend he'd never bought it in the first place. Only he wasn't very good at fooling himself.

So what did he do now? Give it to her? He knew what she would think, what it would mean to her. That he thought she mattered, and she didn't. She couldn't. To care about someone meant to risk that person destroying him. He'd already nearly died once because of a woman—he saw no need to do it again.

Willow cut up vegetables for the salad. Marina opened the oven for the four hundredth time and stared at the bread.

"Is it browning? It doesn't look like it's browning," Maria said.

Julie looked at Willow, then rolled her eyes. "You're the science whiz in this family," she said. "So you're the one who should know that every time you open the oven, you're letting out heat. At this rate, the poor thing is never going to brown. Close the door and step away from the oven."

"I know." Marina did as her sister had said. "But I've never baked bread before. I want it to turn out right."

Willow looked at the bowls and measuring cups stacked in the sink. "What got into you?"

"We're having all our favorites for dinner. I thought homemade bread would be a nice addition."

It was Saturday and Willow and her sisters were at their mother's house. Naomi was off volunteering at yet another low-cost clinic with Dr. Greenberg, so her daughters had decided they would provide dinner.

Willow put down her knife and wiped her hands on a towel. She faced Julie and Marina. "I have an announcement."

They both looked at her.

"My comic strip deal was canceled."

"Oh, no." Marina abandoned her post by the oven and rushed to Willow's side. "How horrible. Why would they do that? When did this happen? Are you all right?"

Julie moved close and put her arm around Willow. "This sucks the big one. Want me to sue them?"

Willow let herself soak up the love and concern, then shook her head. "I'm good. It was a shock and I was crushed at first, but now I'm okay with it. I realized this was an opportunity for me to figure out what I really want to do with my life."

"Which is?" Marina sounded tentative, as if she wasn't sure she wanted to know.

"Working in a nursery at first, then later, opening my own. I start a new job on Monday working at this great place. It's huge. They sell to lots of landscapers, so there are regular plants, but also lots of exotics. Beverly wants me to help her with some hybrids, which will be lots of fun. I'm also starting community college in January. I'm going to take business classes. Eventually I want to open my own nursery."

Marina and Julie stared at her.

"It sounds as if you have it all figured out," Marina said admiringly. "I'm impressed."

"Me, too," Julie told her. "This is a big deal."

"It's not yet, but it will be. I've always sort of fallen into things. This time I'm setting out on a specific direction, heading for somewhere I want to go."

"I'm glad," Julie said. "What happened to generate this change?"

"Losing the syndication deal was hard," Willow admitted. "I had to do a lot of thinking about what I really wanted."

Kane had helped. Actually he'd been the one to push her in the right direction, but oddly, she didn't want to talk about him. She'd always been so willing to go on and on about the men in her life, but he was different. Maybe because she didn't fully understand him yet. Maybe because she wasn't sure if they had an actual relationship. Maybe because just thinking about him made the day seem brighter and she wasn't willing to share that yet.

"There's just one thing," she said, patting Marina on the arm.

"Anything," her sister said with a smile.

"Oh, good. Well, I'm going to need you to marry Todd. The million dollars would be really helpful for start-up capital."

Eight

Kane pulled a flash drive out of his shirt pocket and set it on Todd's desk.

"We have a problem."

Todd picked up the flash drive. "I'm not going to like this problem, am I?"

"Probably not. The new start-up has a lot of proprietary software and that's all they have. We lose that and we might as well shut down. Obviously there will be firewalls and employee agreements in place, but that's not enough. Someone with a couple of these in his or her pocket can steal enough to destroy the company."

"Can you make the company secure?" Todd asked.

"Of course, but it won't be cheap and it's going to require a hell of a lot of logistics and processes."

"That's why you get paid the big bucks."

Kane smiled. "So they tell me. It's a challenge. I enjoy a good challenge."

Todd passed back the flash drive. "You're happy here, working with Ryan and me?"

Kane eyed his boss. What was up? Todd wasn't about to get all touchy-feely, was he? "Why do you ask?"

"You're good. We don't want to lose you. I know you get a lot of offers to go back out in the field or whatever you call it."

Black ops. Secret assignments in dark places in the world protecting idiots who shouldn't be there in the first place.

"I'm not tempted," Kane told him.

"Isn't the money good enough?"

"It's okay. Here I get in on the ground floor on start-ups. That's good money, too."

"I'm going to pry here, but don't you have enough to retire a couple of times over?" Todd asked. "You don't have to keep doing this."

Eight million, Kane thought. Per his last statement. He wanted at least double that before he took off for his isolated paradise.

"I like what I do. Besides, I have expensive tastes. I'll be around for a while."

"That's what I want to hear. But you're seriously not tempted by going back into the field?"

"It's a zero sum game," Kane told him. "Sooner or later someone always gets dead. I got tired of wondering if it was going to be me."

"You don't enjoy the thrill of the chase or the hunt or whatever?"

"Not anymore."

"Good to know." Todd studied him for a minute. "How's Willow?"

"Why do you ask?"

"I just wondered. I saw her car there a couple of nights ago. Are you two…"

"No," Kane said quickly. "We're not together." They couldn't be. He didn't do relationships. Yet he'd invited her into his bed a second time. He wanted her to stay the night and he was looking forward to seeing her again. If that wasn't a relationship, what was it?

"It's interesting," Todd said. "Men, women. Look at Ryan, who a few months ago I would have sworn was as much a cynical bastard as I am when it comes to matters of the heart. But not anymore. He's crazy about Julie. I've never seen him so happy."

"Envious?" Kane asked.

"No. I've been burned enough times not to be tempted anymore. I have no plans to get married. When I'm old, I'll get a bunch of dogs or fish or something and leave all my money to them—just to shake things up."

Kane chuckled. "No one is going to believe that."

"I know, but talking about it tortures my relatives. Especially Aunt Ruth. I should be old enough not to enjoy that, but every now and then I have some fun. Still, she's determined to marry me off."

There was frustration in Todd's voice, but also affection. Kane knew both he and Ryan were close to their aunt.

"Julie isn't a threat anymore," Kane said, remembering the offer of a million dollars to one of the Nelson sisters if she would only marry Todd.

"I'm wondering if Willow is, as well," Todd said.

Kane ignored that. "You still have to deal with Marina."

"I don't know anything about her except I'm going to stay away from her."

"She's a lot like her sisters," Kane said.

"You met her?"

"Once." When she'd come to Willow's rescue, bringing cat supplies and food.

"Attractive?"

Not nearly as beautiful as Willow, but otherwise, "Uh-huh."

"Not that it matters," Todd muttered. "What was Ruth thinking, offering them all that money to marry me? If I wanted to get married, I would."

"Maybe she's trying to help things along."

"Push, not help. Still, I'm younger, stronger and more determined. But if you see Marina hanging around here, you'll let me know?"

"Absolutely."

Kane headed back to his office. He walked into the open space to find a well-dressed older woman waiting for him.

"You must be Kane," she said.

"Ma'am."

She rose and walked toward him. "Please. Not ma'am, I beg you. I'm Ruth Jamison, Willow's grandmother."

Because the cats weren't enough of an invasion, he thought as he shook hands and then offered the woman a seat on the leather sofa in the corner.

When she'd refused anything to drink, he perched in a chair across from her. "How can I help you?" he asked, although he had a bad feeling he already knew the subject matter that had inspired the visit.

"You seem like a nice, direct young man, so I'll be direct as well. I understand you're dating my granddaughter, Willow."

Kane opened his mouth, then closed it. It had been a whole lot easier to deflect Todd than this old woman.

"I know her," he said.

"Yes, most intimately, I've heard." Ruth held up one

hand. "I had lunch with Julie the other day and she mentioned something. I'm not spying. I learned my lesson about getting too involved in my granddaughters' lives. I'm staying out of things. It's my fault we don't really know each other and I have to be patient. I can't force closeness in a few weeks. Still, I was curious about you and curiosity isn't meddling."

Kane had no idea what to say to that. Fortunately Ruth seemed comfortable carrying on the entire conversation.

"I'm beginning to think none of my granddaughters are going to want to marry Todd though of course I'm delighted about Julie and Ryan. As I don't know you at all, I'm not clear if you'll be good for Willow or not. Do you think you have any plans to break up soon?"

"We're not… I haven't…" He swore silently. "I don't know," he said at last.

"Pity. Still, if you're a good man, that could work out. Of course that leaves only Marina for Todd and I have no idea how to get them together. Now that he knows my plan, he'll be on his guard."

"I thought you weren't going to meddle."

"I'm not. I'm helping things along. Young people need that sort of assistance. If I waited for nature to take its course, I'd be dead long before I saw any great-grandchildren. No one wants that."

She rose. "It was lovely to meet you, Kane. Take good care of Willow. She's a very special young woman."

Ruth walked toward the door, then glanced back at him. "I understand you have kittens."

"Ah, yes. Three."

"Good. When they're old enough, I'll take one. I've always wanted a cat. Fraser was never fond of pets, but as I only answer to myself these days, I can have one." She sighed. "One of the few advantages of being alone. Still, if I could have him back…" She shrugged. "Goodbye, Kane."

"Goodbye, Mrs. Jamison."

Willow carried the grocery bags from her car to Kane's front door. "I brought food," she said as she pushed past him into the house.

"So I see."

She walked straight to the kitchen and started to make herself at home. After putting the cold things in the refrigerator, she set the bread and wine on the counter, then turned to face her possibly reluctant host.

"I did phone and tell you I was stopping by with dinner," she said, trying not to sound defensive, when she was actually kind of nervous.

"I got the message."

Yes, well, when her call had gone straight to voice mail, she'd decided to take advantage of the situation and invite herself over.

"It's a celebration," she said.

"You mentioned that in the message."

He didn't look all that happy, but then Kane wasn't a "grin like a fool" kind of guy. On the bright side, he didn't look *unhappy,* either.

"I wanted to say thank you," she said quietly. "For helping me through a rough time when I found out I'd lost my syndication deal and for pointing me in a more positive direction." She smiled. "I just finished my first week working for Beverly and I love it." She held up her hands.

He raised his eyebrows. "Ten fingers. Always a good thing."

"No, silly. My nails. Look. I don't have any. Not long ones, anyway. And I'm getting calluses. I spend my day grubbing around with plants. I couldn't be happier and it's all because of you."

He went from not unhappy to uncomfortable. "You would have figured it out on your own."

"Maybe. But it could have taken me forever. This is what I should have been doing all along and I know that now because of you. Hence the celebration."

One side of his mouth turned up. "Hence?"

"It's a word."

"Not one usually found in this century."

"I'm eclectic."

"Is that what they're calling it?"

He was teasing her, which meant he wasn't upset. Kane wouldn't bother to think twice about tossing her out on her butt if he didn't want her here, which meant he did. A warm glow began in her belly and spread out to her ten fingers and toes.

"I was in New York last week," he said.

"I know that."

"Right. You looked after the cat."

She studied him. Something wasn't right. Kane looked…awkward. But he was always confident, always in charge. How was that possible?

"I appreciate that you came over and dealt with her," he said.

"Jasmine?"

"Right. So, I, ah, got you something."

She felt a great shift in the space-time continuum. Her insides fluttered just a little. "You bought me something? Like a present?"

"A thank-you gift."

She felt like a five-year-old on Christmas morning. "What is it? Is it big? Is it something New York-y?

She waited expectantly while he disappeared into the rear of the house. It was all she could do not to follow him and grab whatever it was. But she forced herself to at least pretend to be mature. Still, a present was very cool.

He returned with a massive gift bag, which he passed to her. She set it on the counter and reached inside.

She had no idea what to expect, but it wasn't a beautiful leather tote with floral appliqués done in a rainbow of colors.

"It's gorgeous," she said, not able to believe this was for her. It had to have cost a fortune. The designer name alone caused her to consciously keep her lips pressed together so her mouth didn't hang open.

"I thought with the flowers and everything, you'd like it."

She looked inside. There were compartments for pens and a cell phone and sunglasses. The lining felt as soft as lingerie, while the leather itself was smooth and buttery.

"This is amazing," she breathed, "but it's too everything." She looked at him. "Kane, this is way more than a 'thanks for looking after my cat' gift."

"It's what I got you. If you like it, then keep it."

"Like it? I'll probably insist on being buried with it."

"Good." He smiled. "I saw the bag and I thought of you. That's why I got it."

He'd thought of her? As in she'd been on his mind while he'd been traveling? That little bit of information was actually just as thrilling as the gift itself.

"Thank you," she said. "Seriously, it's so beautiful and I love it."

"Good. What's the wine?" he asked.

Not the smoothest change in subject, she thought humorously. But very Kane-like. Based on what she knew about his life, he didn't buy many women presents. That would require them to be around more than a day.

Did that mean she was getting to him a little? That she was starting to mean something? She was torn between hope and the need to protect her heart.

She handed him the wine bottle. "A lovely Merlot and on sale with my club card, so I'm a happy camper."

He opened a drawer. From it he pulled some fancy cork puller thingie that just zipped the cork right out.

"Cool," she breathed.

He poured them each a glass of wine.

"Were those steaks I saw you putting into my refrigerator?" he asked as he handed her a glass.

"Uh-huh. You have a barbecue on the patio. I know what you're thinking, but meat cooked on a barbecue doesn't count."

"Of course not," he murmured. "Everybody knows that."

She grinned and touched her glass to his. "To our dreams. May they all come true."

Later, when they were finished with dinner and sitting in the living room in front of a fire, Willow curled up in her chair and tried not to read too much into the evening. Kane had bought her a present, they'd shared wine, a bottle of his after they'd finished hers, had a great dinner and plenty of conversation. They were a man and a woman who had been lovers more than once. In some circles, this could be considered a date. While she wanted it to be, she had a feeling Kane wouldn't agree with her assessment.

The problem was, she liked him. A lot. He was all tough on the outside, but inside, he was a soft cream center.

"For a vegetarian, you like a good steak," he said.

"I know it's a flaw. I can be good for months and months, then every now and then I get a serious craving."

"I would have thought you'd lean more toward fish or chicken."

"That makes more sense," she admitted. "But I tend to jump in with both feet. I love steak. And Dodger Dogs, because what's a baseball game at Dodger Stadium without them?"

"A much smaller experience."

"Exactly."

She smiled at him. He didn't smile back, but there was an expression in his eyes—a heat—that filled her with contentment and more than a little need. She had a sudden vision of them making love in front of the fire.

Of course there were logistical problems. With the kittens now climbing around and trying to get out of their box, it was a little too much like having an audience.

"You want me again," she said happily. "Wanting me is one of your best qualities."

"You're assuming."

"Not really. I can see it in your eyes. They get bright with a kind of fire. It's pretty thrilling. I get all tingly inside and start thinking about taking off my clothes."

His gaze narrowed. "You're drunk."

She looked at her glass and didn't have a clue as to how many she'd already had.

"Tipsy, maybe. Extremely mellow." She giggled. "How can you tell?"

"I doubt you'd talk about the fire in my eyes if you were sober. Or getting naked."

"Oh. Good point. You're logical and straightforward in your thinking. I like that. It's so macho. I suspect a cross-section of my brain would look like a kaleidoscope. Very beautiful and intriguing, but not much world order."

"No one wants you to change."

"Does no one include you?"

"Yes."

Ooh, that sounded promising—although promising for what? She'd lost her train of thought.

"You kept the cats," she said, watching the kittens cuddle against their mother. "I'm glad. You need life in your life." She giggled. "I mean you need something else alive in your life."

"Does this happen often?" he asked, pointing at the glass.

"Almost never. I don't like being out of control. It's too scary. But here, with you, I'm completely safe. It's so strange. You're the only person who has ever made me feel special and safe. Like I can resist that."

"Don't trust me, Willow. I'm not one of the good guys."

"Of course you are. You'd never hurt me. Not physically, anyway. Emotionally, I'm not sure. There could be a good trampling in my future, but it will be worth it."

She had a feeling she was saying too much, but she couldn't figure out how to stop talking. Besides, if he wasn't a good guy, why was he trying to warn her off.

He stood and crossed to her chair, then held out his hand and pulled her to her feet. After setting her wineglass on the table, he stared into her eyes.

"We're not dating," he said.

"Of course not."

"This isn't going anywhere."

"Can I hum while you say all this, because it kind of feels like it needs a soundtrack."

He sighed. "Are you sober enough to make a rational decision about staying the night?"

Ah. At last they were getting somewhere good. "No, but I'm sober enough to say take me hard, big guy."

He pulled her into his arms. "That works for me."

Nine

It was, Willow thought happily as she left the bathroom and sauntered toward the kitchen, a perfect day. If this were a cartoon, little forest animals would be running around and collecting her clothes after making a flower wreath for her hair.

"So you're a morning person," Kane said. He stood by the counter, making coffee. He'd pulled on jeans and a T-shirt. She happened to know for a fact there was nothing on under either.

Of course she was a little scantily clad herself. In the absence of a robe, he'd offered a clean white dress shirt. It was ridiculously big on her, but she liked wearing it anyway. Wearing his shirt felt intimate.

"I sometimes enjoy the morning," she said, unable to look away from his face. He was better looking now than when she'd first met him. She wasn't sure if that was because he was more relaxed, or because she was getting to know him.

"Are you tired?" he asked.

"Oh, yeah. You?"

"I'll nap later."

She laughed at the thought of Kane napping and at the pleasure of knowing he felt comfortable enough with her to joke around.

He pushed the button on the coffeemaker, then walked over, bent down and kissed her.

She surrendered to his embrace, letting her body ease into his. His hands slipped under his shirt to rest on her bare butt.

"Again?" she asked as her blood heated.

"You'll be sore."

"I'm a big, tough girl. I can handle it."

He kissed her again and stepped back. "Maybe after breakfast."

He meant coffee, she thought with a grin. Kane didn't keep much food around. He was such a guy, she thought affectionately. But a really good one. Sure he was tough and dangerous, but not to her. With her, he was gentle and kind and funny. He made love to her with a thoroughness that left her quivering from the inside out.

"You're smiling," he said.

"I was thinking about last night."

"Okay."

She laughed. "Now you look like a lion after the kill. Very self-satisfied."

"I didn't kill you."

"I'm not sure about that. I distinctly remember dying a few times…from the pleasure."

The fire returned to his eyes and she felt an answering need inside. But more important than that was his smile.

He relaxed around her. She knew enough to wonder if that ever happened around anyone else.

"So you must be hungry," he said. "For breakfast."

"Starved."

He motioned to the refrigerator.

She rolled her eyes. "Oh, please. I know what's in there. A few condiments and a box of baking soda."

His expression turned smug. "You think you know everything."

"I do. The government often contacts me to help them out of difficult situations because of that." She walked to the refrigerator and pulled it open. Inside she found…food.

She stared at it for a second, then looked at Kane.

"You went to the grocery store," she said.

He shrugged. "While you were still sleeping."

"You have food in here. You hate food."

"I like food just fine. I knew how you felt about eating, and I had a feeling you'd be back, so I got a few things."

She looked at the carton of eggs, the package of vegan bacon, cheese, English muffins, juice, not to mention bread, lunch meat, a bag of salad and cookie dough. This was for more than just a single breakfast, she thought as she closed the door and stared at Kane.

"You thought I'd be back?" she asked, wondering if she could dare read any significance into that statement.

"You're stubborn."

She moved in front of him and placed her hands on his chest. "You're a big, tough guy. You could keep me away if you really wanted to."

He sighed. "Willow, don't make too much of this."

"Stop saying that to me. You invite me in with one hand and push me away with the other. So here's the thing." She sucked in a breath and braced herself for the explosion.

"We're dating," she told him. "You can call it what you want, but that's the truth. We're an item, a couple, a set, a pair. Whatever. You want to keep seeing me and I want to keep seeing you. That's dating. Welcome to the real world."

The fire fled his eyes and his expression hardened, but he didn't back away. So that was something. Then he covered her hands with his and pulled them away from his body.

"There's a reason I don't do this," he told her.

"Do what?"

"Date."

"Okay. Hit me." She smiled. "That's slang for tell me what you mean."

He narrowed his gaze. "I do slang."

"I wasn't sure. You nondaters can be so tricky."

He ignored that. "Getting involved requires trust, and I don't trust anyone. It requires change and I don't change."

He was so wrong, she thought, feeling sad for his inability to see the truth. Whatever he might tell himself, he *did* trust her. He never would have given her the key to his house otherwise. How hard would it have been to take Jasmine and her kittens to the pound? But he hadn't.

As for the not changing issues, from where she stood—which was deliciously close to Kane—he already had changed. The gift he'd brought her from New York. The food in the refrigerator. Hello, all big changes.

But instead of saying that, she murmured, "Don't worry. Dating me is fairly simple. There are only a few rules and you're a pretty bright guy. I think you can handle them."

Then she held her breath because she knew this could go either way. Kane could accept her offer or he could throw her out. Honestly, she had no idea which way it would fall.

He stared into her eyes. "What are the rules?"

Relief poured through her, although with enough happiness to make her float. "Let me just start by saying I'm a fabulous girlfriend. I'm going to spoil you for everyone else."

"I think I can handle that."

"Good. Okay—I want you to call when you say you're going to call, show up on time, not see anyone else."

He still held her hands in his. Now he pulled her close and rubbed her fingers. "I'm not interested in anyone else."

She nearly purred. Talk about exactly what she wanted to hear. "I'm glad. Let's see. What else? Oh, compliments. Compliments are always welcome."

"And gifts?" he asked.

"Not required. But I wouldn't say no." She grinned. "But where you're concerned, I rarely say no."

His eyes darkened with an emotion she couldn't read. "I'm not good at this, Willow. You're asking a lot."

"I have every faith in you."

"What happens when this goes badly?"

"Why assume the worst? What happens when it goes well?"

He released her hand and stroked her face. "Such an optimist. You should get that looked at."

"I have a bubbly personality—it's part of my charm."

"Yes, it is." He kissed her. "Stay right there."

He left the kitchen. She watched him go, then poured two cups of coffee and waited for his return.

When he walked toward her, he held out a business card. "My work number. I wrote my cell number on the back."

She took the card and knew what he was offering— access to his world. Access to him. If things did go badly— as he expected—her having this information could make his life messy. It was a big step for him.

In return, she gave him her heart. She wasn't sure it could be considered a fair trade.

Late Sunday morning Willow stood in front of the second biggest house she'd ever seen. It was three stories of elegant trim and windows and formal grounds. There had to be at least three people on the permanent gardening staff.

Marina joined her and linked arms. "So, what do you think?"

"It's amazing. I can't believe we're related to anyone who lives here. Todd's house is bigger, but we don't really know him, so it doesn't count. You think she has live-in help?"

"I'm sure of it."

"I don't think I'd like that. I'd want to come and go without being monitored. Plus, what about walking around naked? Kind of embarrassing with staff."

Marina laughed. "How much time do you spend being naked in your house?"

"Not much, but I want to keep the option open."

Julie hurried up to join them. "Sorry I'm late. I was, um, busy and didn't noticed the time."

Willow looked at Marina. "I'm guessing she means she and Ryan were doing the wild thing again."

"Oh, yeah."

Julie smoothed the front of her dress. "I'm ignoring you two. Come on…let's go see what our grandmother has in store for us."

As they walked toward the front of the house, Marina sighed. "You're still seeing Kane, aren't you?"

Willow smiled. "Uh-huh. It's official. We're an item."

"Great. So everyone has someone but me. That's kind of depressing."

Julie patted Marina's arm. "You can have Todd."

"Gee, thanks."

The three of them laughed, then Willow pushed the bell by the door.

"Is there a maid?" Marina asked in a low voice.

"In a uniform," Julie whispered back. "You'll love it."

There wasn't just a maid—there was a staff. Someone to show them in, someone else to bring them drinks, a third person to serve the meal.

Willow did her best to keep her attention on the food and the conversation, but she was distracted by the beauty of the "breakfast room."

"So much brighter and less formal than the dining room," Grandmother Ruth had said as she'd led the sisters into it.

If this was informal, Willow didn't think she was ready for anything more grand.

Six beveled glass windows opened onto a beautiful English-style formal garden. There were three crystal chandeliers hanging over the inlaid table and two matching buffets on the wall. The carpet looked antique, the artwork original and the china probably cost more per place setting than she made in a week.

"How are your wedding plans coming?" Ruth asked as the maid set down salad plates in front of each of them.

Julie looked up surprised. "Ah, well, fine. We haven't done much in the way of planning."

"Oh, are you waiting until after the baby's born?" Ruth asked.

Julie touched her stomach. "No, but I've been busy with work."

"And Ryan," Marina teased. "How could details like place cards and vows be more interesting than him?"

Julie grinned. "Excellent point."

Ruth cleared her throat. "I hope this doesn't sound too presumptuous, my dear, but I would be honored if you would consider having the wedding here. The backyard is beautiful, even this time of year, and there's plenty of room for a large tent or two. As an alternative, depending on the size of the wedding, we could hold it inside. There's actually a huge ballroom on the third floor. I never go up there, but it's quite lovely. I know a few wedding planners who could turn the space into a fairyland or whatever else you'd like."

Willow eyed her sister. She'd heard how Ruth had meddled in Julie's relationship with Ryan. But in the end, the old woman had come through, telling her granddaughter she only wanted Julie's happiness.

Willow guessed the offer was as much a way to connect as a desire to see her oldest granddaughter married in her house.

Nothing about this place was her style, but Julie might like it. It was a once-in-a-lifetime opportunity.

Julie smiled at her grandmother. "I'd have to talk it over with Ryan. If he's willing, I'd be very interested in holding the wedding here."

"Wonderful. You will be totally in charge. I won't get involved, except to pay the bills."

"No," Julie said quickly. "You don't have to do that. We want to pay for things ourselves."

"You're my granddaughter and he's my great-nephew. We're all family, dear. It will be my gift to you both."

Marina leaned toward Willow. "Think she'd spring for new cars for us single sisters?" she asked in a whisper.

Willow grinned. "I'm sure they're there for the asking."

Ruth glanced at Willow. "How is your young man? Kane?"

"I, ah, he's good." She tried to figure out if her grand-mother should know about Kane. It was possible Todd or Ryan had mentioned she was dating him, assuming they knew. Well, Todd should know. He could see her car parked by Kane's place.

"Interesting man," Ruth said. "Dangerous, which is always exciting and sexy."

Willow nearly choked on her bite of lettuce. Had her sixtysomething grandmother just said sexy?

"He's very wealthy, you know," Ruth added. "An impressive investment portfolio."

Willow's eyes widened. "How do you know?"

"Todd mentioned it. He didn't give me exact figures, but apparently Kane doesn't work because he has to."

Willow disagreed. However much money Kane had now, he didn't think it was enough. Apparently privacy and a secure location didn't come cheap.

Would he really do it, she wondered. Would he really leave everyone behind and go off by himself? The thought of it made her sad—not only because his leaving would devastate her but because she didn't think it would make him happy. Sometime in his past he'd gotten the idea that he had to be solitary. She didn't think that was true anymore, but she wasn't sure she could convince him otherwise.

"He seems very responsible," Ruth continued. "An excellent quality in a man. Although he's a bit of a loner. You'll have to watch that. Some men like that can be turned around, but others can't. Be sure he's given his heart before you risk your own."

Excellent advice, Willow thought. Unfortunately it was about a month too late. Kane pretty much had possession of her heart from the moment he'd fussed over her ankle, taken in Jasmine and her kittens, then freaked when Jasmine went off for a little alone time.

He might have the rest of the world fooled into thinking he was a big, tough soldier, but she happened to know that inside he was warm and caring. He was also the man she loved.

Julie leaned toward her grandmother. "This would be you staying out of things?" she asked with a smile.

"Oh, no. I'm meddling, aren't I?" Ruth sighed. "Old habits and all that. But I do have one more thing before I swear off the habit forever."

Julie laughed. "Of course you do. What is it?"

Ruth turned to Marina. "I would so like for you to meet Todd. I know you have every reason to be apprehensive and so I'll even withdraw the offer of money, if you'd like. Please?"

Marina looked at her sisters, then back at Ruth. "Okay, I'll meet him, but only if the money offer stays on the table. The promise of riches makes it all the more interesting."

"You sure about that?" Julie asked. "What if you like him? The money will get in the way. Trust me, it's a complication."

"Oh, please. No offense, Grand, but what are the odds of that happening? I doubt he's my type. So I'll meet him, just to make you happy, but don't have any expectations."

"You're tempting fate," Willow murmured.

"I'll risk it," Marina said. "What chance is there that Todd Aston the Third is the one for me?"

"Unfortunately she's right," Ruth said. "But I'll still hold on to my grandmother dreams. It's all about family, isn't it? Oh, speaking of family, I'll be meeting your father next weekend and I'm looking forward to that."

"Me, too," Marina said.

Julie only looked annoyed, while Willow wondered what her father would have to say to her this time.

Later, when lunch was over, the sisters left. When they'd reached their cars, Marina turned to Julie.

"Are you really considering having your wedding here?" she asked.

Julie grinned. "Sure. Ryan loves Ruth, so he'd be happy. I'm sure Ruth knows the best party planners around, so that will make things easier. I'm not letting her pay for everything, but other than that, I think it's a great idea. You don't approve?"

"I like the idea," Marina admitted. "The house is gorgeous. I think it's a beautiful venue and if it makes Grand happy, then hey. Why not?"

"Willow?" Julie asked.

"I like the idea, too. Imagine how great the pictures would be. And it is a chance to bond with Ruth. You two got off to a rocky start."

"All forgiven," Julie said.

"Speaking of forgiven," Marina murmured. "Are you okay? About Dad coming home, I mean."

Julie shrugged. "I don't know. I guess. I've been talking to Ryan a lot and that's helped. Mom loves him. I may not understand her feelings, but I want to respect them. He's her husband and our father and in his own useless, selfish, twisted way, a part of the family."

Marina grinned. "As long as you're respecting everyone's feelings."

Julie sucked in a deep breath. "I'm doing my best to keep an open mind, okay? That's as good as it's going to get. In my heart, I'm still angry with him for what he's done to Mom for the past twenty years and I'm furious with her for putting up with it. But it's her decision. Not mine. I love her and I acknowledge that he's my father. That is my peak maturity experience for the day. Anyone expecting more is going to be disappointed."

"You'll get there," Marina said. "Personally I can't wait to see him."

"You always were his favorite," Julie said easily.

"Not his favorite, but we get along. I agree that life would have been better if he'd been the kind of guy to stick around, but he's not. So I accept him for what he is and enjoy the time he's around."

"You're a better person than I'll ever be," Julie said with a sigh. "I have to run. I'm meeting Ryan." She waved and walked to her car.

Marina turned to Willow. "I suppose you want to get back to Kane?"

"Pretty much."

"Wow—both my sisters seriously involved. I suppose that means I need to find myself a guy."

"You have Todd."

Marina laughed. "Right. All I can think is that our lone date will be a night I'll never get back." She hugged Willow. "See you at Mom's."

"I'll be there."

Marina left.

Willow climbed into her car and started the engine. Now that she was alone, she could stop pretending she was excited about her father's return. Her guilty secret had always been that she dreaded his visits. It never mattered what she did or how she tried, he never saw her as anything but a failure.

As a child, she'd tried desperately to make her father

proud of her. Tried and failed countless times. A few years ago, she'd stopped trying. But that didn't mean the hurt had gone away.

Ten

Willow shifted in the passenger seat of Kane's Mercedes. Normally the yummy smell of a leather interior and a dashboard that looked more like a cockpit would have distracted her. If nothing else, she would have tried to justify *how* the smell of leather could be yummy when she didn't eat meat, except on very special occasions when it didn't count.

But this afternoon, she couldn't seem to think about any of that. Instead she fought against the rising need to throw up and wondered if the knot of dread in her stomach would ever go away.

"You're quiet," Kane said as he pulled into the left turn lane and glanced at her. "I've learned that's not always a good thing."

"I'm fine. Okay, not fine, but not awful. Semiawful, maybe. This is all a mistake. Why are we doing this? We shouldn't be doing this. I should have said no or that we were busy or at least that you were busy. Asking you along was a mistake."

She bit her lip and sighed. "I don't mean that in a bad way."

"Oh, no. I'm tingling from the thrill of the compliment."

That made her smile. "You're not a tingle kind of guy."

"You can't be sure about that."

"If I had a lot of money, I'd bet it all. Anyway, the not inviting you was about me. I'm nervous. Besides, you don't do family stuff. Why did you say yes?"

He made the turn. "Because you asked and it seemed important to you."

Under other circumstances his words would have thrilled her. She would have felt an honest-to-goodness flutter right in the center of her chest. But not today. The dread was too big and growing and this was all going to be a disaster.

"It's my dad," she admitted. "He's back and while that's a good thing, it's also…confusing."

"Parents can be that way."

"Do you remember yours?" she asked.

He shrugged. "Not my dad. I never knew him. I'm not sure my mom knew who he was. I have a few fuzzy memories of her. She was strung out most of the time, or gone. She died when I was eight."

He spoke the words easily, as if he'd long made peace with them. But how was that possible?

"Where was Social Services in all this?" she asked. "Why didn't they come get you?"

"I don't think they knew about me. When my mom died, I went out on the streets. I'd been living there most of the time anyway. I was already like a mascot to a few gang members. It wasn't a big step to be accepted by all of them. Besides, I made myself useful. I ran errands—delivering drugs, picking up money."

He might as well be talking about life on Saturn. "You didn't go to school?"

"Not after junior high."

"But you're obviously educated."

"Got my GED while in the army. When I got into basic training, I realized I knew nothing about anything. I started reading in my spare time. Everything is self-taught."

Which was incredible, she thought. He was a sophisticated, dangerous man of the world who'd started with nothing.

Okay—now her pity party had just taken a turn for the worse. Before she'd been worried about what would happen with her father—what he would say in front of Kane. Now Kane was even more amazing and her humiliation would be greater.

She wanted to tell him about her fears and have him put his arms around her and say it didn't matter. Except she wasn't sure he would. In truth, what she really wanted was for him to say he loved her and, to quote Marina, what were the odds of that happening?

But he liked her. He liked her and he was dating her and Kane didn't date, so that was something. She would hang on to that and pray for a miracle. That she could go one afternoon with her father and not have him say anything hideous.

She felt her eyes burning. As tears were the last thing she wanted to deal with, she drew in a deep breath and changed the subject.

"The kittens are really growing," she said. "They'll need a bigger box."

"I'll get one this week."

She forced herself to think about Jasmine and her beautiful kittens and how precious they all were. That was safe. Kittens and chocolate and how Kane touched her in the night.

The knot loosened a little...right until they pulled up in front of her mother's house.

"We're here," she said, hoping she sounded more excited than she felt.

They walked inside. Everyone else was already there and called out greetings. Her father stood in the center of the group, as always.

He looked the same, Willow thought. Still handsome and blond, with a deep tan and blue eyes that were permanently crinkled in good humor.

"You must be Kane," Jack Nelson said with a grin. "I've heard so much about you."

The two men shook hands.

"How's my Willow?" Jack asked.

"I'm good, Daddy." She stepped into his embrace.

His arms were familiar, as was the uneasy combination of longing and apprehension. She knew the hits were coming. It was just a matter of when and where.

She stepped back, but her father kept his arm around her shoulder.

"This is how it should be," he said. "Back with all my girls."

Willow stepped free of his embrace and walked over to her mother.

"How are you doing?" she asked, although she could see the happiness on her mother's face.

"I'm wonderful. It's so good to have him home."

Willow nodded. She noticed Kane talking to Ryan. Julie stood next to her fiancé, holding on to his hand as if she would never let go. Families were complicated.

"Now let me see if I have this straight," Jack said to Kane. "You work for Ryan here."

Kane nodded. "I run security for the various companies Ryan and Todd are funding."

"Ryan says you're the best in the business."

"I know what I'm doing."

"Impressive." Jack slapped Kane on the back. "Good. Good. At least you're not like Willow's other losers."

"Dad," Marina said quickly, taking her father's hand. "Come on. Let's go into the family room. UCLA is playing University of Washington. We can watch our guys kick their Seattle butts."

Willow appreciated the save, but wished it hadn't been necessary. She felt heat on her cheeks and the knot in her stomach had turned to dread.

Her father allowed himself to be turned away. But at the step down to the family room, he glanced back at Kane.

"I'm glad Willow's moving up. I've always worried about her. She's never been as smart or pretty as her sisters. I wondered who would want her. It's good to know I was wrong."

Willow felt as if she'd been hit with an emotional baseball bat. Her face flamed with embarrassment.

Not knowing what else to do, she fled into the kitchen where she picked up a knife and began cutting bread into slices. As she didn't know what they were having or what her mother wanted the bread for, she could really be messing up the recipe. But she had to be doing something. The bread got all blurry and she couldn't see anything. She tossed the knife down and gave in to the tears.

Then her sisters were there.

"He's such a jerk," Julie muttered as she hugged Willow. "This is only one of the reasons I hate him."

"He's not the most sensitive man," Marina said as she hugged them both. "Willow, I'm so sorry."

Willow let their love surround her. It didn't heal the wound, but it eased a little of the pain. Still, the memory of the humiliation clawed at her. What was Kane thinking?

"I should never have brought him," she whispered. "I can't do this."

Instead of answering, her sisters moved away. For a second, she was alone, then strong arms encircled her.

She didn't have to open her eyes to recognize the man. Indecision tore at her. While she needed to be with him, she was too embarrassed to want to face him.

"I'm sorry," she said, forcing herself to look into his eyes.

But instead of censure, she saw something that looked very much like affection.

"You can't pick your parents."

"I know. He's always been like that. Do you want to leave? I could get a ride home with Marina."

He brushed away her tears, then bent down and kissed her. Really kissed her. There was heat and need and plenty of tongue. When they resurfaced, her head was fuzzy and it had nothing to do with feeling bad.

"I want you," he breathed. "I want you naked. I want to make love with you until we're both exhausted. Then I want to talk to you and be with you. Just you, Willow. You know how I feel about relationships, yet here I am. With you. I've known a lot of women and you are unique in more ways than I can count. You are passionate and beautiful and stubborn and giving and you delight me."

The knot disappeared. Her tears dried up and she wanted to crawl inside Kane and live there forever.

She loved him. The words hovered on her tongue, then she swallowed them. Kane was many things, but open to being loved wasn't one of them. It didn't seem fair to repay his kindness with a statement that would terrify him.

But soon, she thought. Soon.

Kane watched the dynamics of the Nelson family and felt more uncomfortable by the second. If intimacy was a dance, then everyone in this house had forgotten the steps. Julie clung to Ryan as if he were the only point of safety. Willow put on a brave face, but he saw the pain behind her big eyes and it made him want to hit something…or someone. Marina seemed the only one able to hang out with her father and be relaxed, while Naomi, the girls' mother, fluttered from place to place in an attempt to make peace.

He'd already berated himself for ever agreeing to join Willow at her less than happy family reunion. He knew better, yet she'd asked and he'd said yes. Because he found it difficult to deny her anything.

He was losing it, he thought. He had it bad for a woman and he knew the trouble that led to. Getting involved could get a man dead.

"Kane!" Jack said jovially. "Come join me in my study."

Kane would rather have been air-dropped into a piranha-filled river, but he nodded and followed the other man through the family room and into a bookcase-lined study. Jack shut the door behind him.

"I love all the women in my life, but sometimes a man needs to get away." Jack grinned. "You know what I mean?"

Kane took one of the leather chairs as his host poured them each a Scotch.

Jack stretched out in the recliner opposite Kane's and raised his glass. "To my ladies. May they always welcome me home."

Kane didn't acknowledge the toast. What was the point

of making trouble? The visit would end and then he and Willow would leave.

Jack sighed. "Do I have a great life, or what? I love this house. I'm always happy to get back here. Naomi's a terrific woman. So warm and welcoming. She understands me. The patience of a saint, that woman. And the girls are special. I'm willing to admit I would have liked a son, of course. What man wouldn't, but maybe it's better this way."

Kane sipped the Scotch. It was single malt, eighteen years old. He knew what the bottle had cost and doubted it had fit comfortably in Naomi's food budget.

"It is better," Kane said casually. "The way you take off and abandon your family every time you get an itch, there could be trouble. A son would grow up and beat the crap out of you."

Jack stared at him. "It's not like that."

"It's exactly like that."

Jack shrugged. "Tell me about your job. Do you like working for Ryan? Weren't you in the military before? Isn't this a little boring for you?"

"I was in Special Forces," Kane said after he put his glass on the small table beside his chair. "Nearly nine years. I specialized in the undetected kill. Get in, get the job done, get out before anyone knows you're there. I was good at it, too."

Jack swallowed. "Excellent. Excellent."

"From there I went into private security. That's the polite word for it. Basically, I was a mercenary for hire. I've survived the most dangerous places in the world. There's a lot of money in that kind of work."

"I can imagine." Jack shifted in his chair. "If I ever need a second career, eh?"

Kane stood and looked down at the older man. "We're

not friends, Jack. We'll never be friends. I don't like you or respect you, but you're Willow's father and as much as I'd like to change that, I can't. You're an ass. You have a wife who worships you, daughters who adore you and that's not enough for you. You want to go play, so you keep leaving them. Of course they keep taking you back, so they have some responsibility in this, too."

He moved toward the door, then turned back to his host. "If it had been me, I would have kicked your butt a long time ago. Grow up. Be a man. You might find you actually like it. But whatever you decide, don't make Willow cry again. If you do, I'll hunt you down like the snake you are and I'll skin you alive. Are we clear?"

Jack nodded frantically and Kane left the room.

He made his way to the backyard, where he was able to breathe for a few minutes.

But his solitude was short-lived. The door behind him opened again and Naomi stepped out.

"I know I'm interrupting," she said. "I won't take long. I heard what you said to Jack."

Kane held in a groan. Just perfect. He looked at Willow's mother. "Do you want me to apologize?"

"Not at all," she said with a smile. "I was impressed. I know Jack was terrified. I might love the man, but I'm not blind to his flaws. Maybe you'll change him, although I doubt it."

"You could stop welcoming him home," Kane said flatly.

"I could, but I won't. I'd rather have Jack some of the time than never at all. That's my flaw. Still, this isn't about me. I wanted to thank you for defending Willow. I've been on Jack for years about how he talks to her, but he would never listen. I think things are going to be different now."

That was something, Kane thought. "Why her? Why not Julie or Marina?"

Naomi sighed. "Willow had some learning problems when she was younger. Nothing serious, but for a while, school was much harder for her. The doctors said it was just because her brain was wired a little differently. Eventually everything righted itself and she did fine. But Jack can't or won't forget those earlier years. I'm not sure why he thinks Willow isn't as pretty as her sisters, though."

"She's not," Kane told her. "She's prettier by a lot."

Naomi's smiled again. "Not that you're biased."

He shrugged.

"I think Jack sees a lot of himself in Willow," Naomi said. "She's always been the dreamer. Or at least she was. Lately she seems to have found herself in more ways than one. She loves her new job at the nursery."

He thought about the army of plants that was slowly filling his place. "I guessed that."

"I always worried about Willow because of the kind of men she chose. So many troubled souls in need of a good rescue. But I see now she was just filling her time until she found the right sort of man." Naomi touched his arm. "You're everything I could have wished for her. Thank you."

She stepped back into the house.

Kane continued to stand on the porch, looking out on the lush backyard, but not really seeing it. Every cell in his body warned him this situation was dangerous and getting more deadly by the second.

That night Kane lay on his back as Willow cuddled up next to him.

"So did you hate every minute of it?" she asked.

He stroked her pale blond hair. "It wasn't so bad."

"The beginning was a nightmare, but later, things got better. I mentioned my new job to my dad and he was actually supportive. I thought maybe the sky was going to fall, but no, he was just being nice. Maybe he's mellowing."

The happiness and wonder in her voice let him know he'd done the right thing where Jack was concerned. Kane would still like to take the man out back and break a few bones, but polite society frowned on that. Not to mention how Willow would react if she found out he'd hurt her dad. Her mixed feelings wouldn't extend far enough to support actual violence.

"Dinner was good," she added, then went on about the meal.

Kane listened to her sweet voice and felt the wanting take hold of him. It didn't matter that they'd just finished making love—he still needed her again.

Needed. When had he ever needed anyone? Needing, like caring and believing and all those other relationship words got you dead.

She pushed herself up on one elbow and looked down at him. She was naked and her long hair veiled her bare breasts. She was an erotic vision. What the hell had he done to deserve her?

"I want to say something," she told him. "I'm going to say it and then you're going to hold me in your arms. We'll turn out the light and go to sleep. You're not allowed to say anything back. I don't want you to. I mean that. This is about me telling you. Okay?"

Dread chased away desire. Wariness stiffened his muscles and made him ready for flight. He nodded curtly.

She drew in a breath, then smiled. "I love you. I have for a while, but I'm finally ready to say the words. I love you."

She lowered herself back onto his shoulder and closed her eyes. "Night, Kane."

"Good night."

He turned out the light and lay there in his dark. She loved him. It didn't matter whether or not he believed her. *She* believed and that was enough.

How had he let this happen?

Damn stupid question, he thought grimly. He'd let her in and she'd made herself at home. Now she had feelings and expectations and he would never be able to take care of either. He didn't want her love. Not now, not ever.

He knew she'd meant the words as a gift, but to him they were little more than a trap. He could feel the metal teeth holding him in place. It was either break free or die. He sacrificed himself or he sacrificed Willow.

He might pretend to weigh the options, but he already knew what he was going to choose, and how much it would destroy her when he did.

Eleven

Willow fixed coffee the next morning while Kane got ready for work. She was both happy and apprehensive. Although she didn't regret telling him the truth about her feelings and was proud of herself for being so brave, she couldn't help the slight quiver of nerves in her belly. Kane hadn't wanted a girlfriend, let alone someone to love him. How would he react to what she'd said?

She poured coffee into his travel mug just as he walked into the kitchen. She held out the mug and allowed herself a momentary eye-party as she admired his broad shoulders and narrow hips in his tailored suit.

"Morning." He kissed her on the mouth, then took the coffee. "I have a meeting at seven-thirty, so I have to run."

"That's fine. I'll feed Jasmine."

"Great." He kissed her again.

She grabbed the lapels of his suit and stared into his

eyes. "About last night," she began. "Are you okay with what I said?"

"You're always going to lead with your heart, Willow. I wouldn't change that."

Then he was gone. It was only after he'd driven away that she realized he hadn't answered her question.

The shooting range stood in a converted warehouse. It was private and exclusive, catering mostly to those with the money to pay for the best. Kane scanned his membership card, then headed for the scored target room. After checking then loading his Glock, he put on ear protection and stepped into the room.

He could still hear the sound of gunfire and see the flash of the shots. Ignoring the other shooters, he walked to the end of the aisle and faced his target. But instead of seeing the silhouette of a man, he saw Willow. He heard her laughing as she bent down to pick up one of the kittens, caught the curve of a hip as she danced in his kitchen to some Country song. He felt the soft warmth of her skin and the breath of her sigh as he pleasured her.

He lowered his gun and forced himself to focus. He came to the club a couple of times a month to stay sharp. He liked his time here and looked forward to the challenge. But not today. Today there was only Willow.

He drew in a deep breath and forced her from his mind, then lined up his gun with the target and fired six rounds, one after the other.

George, the manager of the place, walked over. "Hey, Kane. Haven't seen you in a while."

"I know. Been busy."

George eyed the target at the far end of the room. "Did you miss one?"

Kane pushed the button to bring the target closer, then swore. Sure enough, one of the bullets had missed the silhouette completely.

"You're not usually off your game," George said. "I guess we'll be seeing more of you."

Kane nodded and the other man left.

The target fluttered slightly as Kane returned it to its original position, then he stared down the barrel of his gun and knew he was in real danger of losing his edge. As that edge was the only thing that had kept him alive, he couldn't risk that.

He didn't have to ask what had happened—he knew exactly what had changed in his life. Or who.

She loved him. She'd spoken the words with a conviction that left him no way out. He had to believe her and that belief changed everything.

She *was* love. Her entire existence defined the word. She was warm and caring and giving and impetuous. She was also strong enough to have faith—something he'd never had the courage for.

To give her what she wanted was impossible. She wanted him to love her back, to need her, to have her in his life forever. The thought of that filled him with both longing and terror. Only the longing surprised him.

Was he tempted? Did he really think he could expose himself that way, be defined by and connected to another person and still survive? Hadn't facing death more times than he could count taught him anything?

He drew in a steadying breath, then faced the target and fired again. This time the shots filled an area not much bigger than a quarter, exactly where the heart would be. Calmness filled him. He knew what was wrong and he knew how to fix it.

In this world, only the strongest survived. He refused to be anything but the one left standing at the end.

Willow arrived at Kane's with yet another plant. This time she had an ailing orchid. Beverly said it was too late to save it, but Willow was sure she would convince the slender bloom to hang on long enough to get strong again.

As she let herself into the house, she was greeted by three very excited kittens.

"You got out of your box," she said as she set the plant on a table, then crouched on the floor. "Look at you. So big and tough."

They ran to her and began to climb all over her. Needle-sharp claws cut through her jeans and raked her skin. She winced and picked up the biggest offender, a gray and white male, with splotches of orange on his face and paws.

"You're a wild thing, aren't you?" She nuzzled the kitten. He purred and rubbed his face against hers.

The tabby female kitten stood on Willow's thighs and batted at her brother's flicking tail.

"You're all so cute," Willow said. "I want to keep you all."

She couldn't, of course. In theory she couldn't have a cat at all. Not at her place. But if she were to have a change in location...

She stretched out on the floor and let the kittens romp around on her. Jasmine came over to get her scratching. Willow let the kitty love wash over her.

Who knew things would work out like this? A couple of months ago, she'd been intent on giving Todd a piece of her mind. Now her entire life was different. She was happy in her work, desperately in love and moving in a totally different direction. Life wasn't just full of surprises...it was very, very good.

She heard a key in the door and smiled expectantly. When Kane walked in, she grinned up at him. "I'm being held hostage by the cats. You're going to have to save me. Think you're up to it, Mr. Big Security Guy?"

But instead of smiling or offering her a hand or even joining her on the floor, Kane closed the door behind him and said, "I'd like to speak with you, please. Can you get up?"

He wasn't smiling. He wasn't doing anything. As she scrambled to her feet, she fought the nagging sense of the familiar. What was it?

And then she knew. It was his eyes. They were empty again. As empty as they'd been when she'd first met him.

"Kane?"

"This is a mistake," he said. "I'm sorry for my part in it. I should never have let you believe there was ever a chance for more. There isn't. I don't want there to be. I am solitary by choice. You can't change that. I'm not interested in what you're offering, Willow. I don't want any of it. Or you."

He spoke calmly, simply and with a clarity that left her bleeding from wounds that would never heal. She couldn't think, couldn't speak, could only try to keep standing.

"I..." she began.

He cut her off. "This isn't negotiable. I'll give you two hours to clear out."

She didn't hurt enough. Willow knew that was a bad sign. There was plenty of pain, but a part of her was still numb. If she could barely survive this, how would she make it when the real ache set in?

"What can I get you?" Marina carried in tea from the kitchen. "Wine? Vodka? A contract on Kane?"

Willow laughed, then sobbed and reached for another

tissue. "I don't want him dead or even hurt. I can't. I love him."

She sat curled up on Marina's sofa. All of Kane's plants were still in her car, but her sister had offered to take in Jasmine and her family until the kittens were old enough to be adopted.

"I'm ok-kay," she said, her voice shaking.

"Oh, sure." Her sister sat next to her and put a hand on her leg. "I can tell."

"It's not that bad yet," Willow told her. "I think it's going to hit me later."

One of the kittens crawled into her lap and curled up, as if offering comfort. Willow patted her.

"It's not his fault," she said. "He t-told me what he was. He was very specific about that. I'm the one who didn't believe him. I just plowed in where I wasn't wanted. Why do I do that? Why don't I listen?"

"We all hear what we want to hear."

Willow shook her head. "It's more than that. I was so proud of myself. I finally felt I'd moved on from rescuing guys, you know? Kane didn't need rescuing. In fact, he rescued me in every way possible." She sniffed. "Isn't that a line from *Titanic?*"

Marina smiled, then stroked her hair. "I'm sure it's okay for you to use it."

"I love sad stories at the movies, but in real life, it really sucks." She blew her nose and reached for another tissue. "I thought I was going to have it all. Isn't that stupid."

"No. Don't say that. It's not stupid. Why wouldn't you have it all?"

Willow sighed. Her body hurt as if she had a bad case of the flu. Her heart ached and every beat seemed almost more effort than it could muster. Her eyes were burning and gritty.

She'd been emotionally beat up and left for dead. The worst part was, she couldn't blame Kane.

"He wasn't wrong," she whispered. "You can't blame him."

"Watch me," Marina said, looking annoyed. "He's a complete bastard. How dare he hurt you like this?"

"But he didn't do anything wrong," Willow reminded her. "He told me the rules and he played by them."

"Why does he get to set the rules? Why not you? Why not me?"

Willow managed a slight smile. "You weren't dating him. As for me, well, I didn't have many rules."

"He changed everything when he agreed to keep seeing you," her sister told her. "He left the scary world he regularly inhabits and entered the world of normal people. Once there, he has to play by our rules and he didn't. Everything was fine until one day he announced he was through and gave no real reason. That's not allowed."

Willow reached for her tea and took a sip. "I told him I loved him. I think that's what set him off."

Marina stared at her. "For real?"

Willow nodded. "He's the one. I've liked other guys and had crushes and all kinds of things, but I've never been in love. Not until Kane. He's so strong and giving and when I'm with him, I feel safe."

She set down her mug and patted the kitten on her lap. "I know being safe doesn't seem like a big deal, but I've never felt much of it before."

"I believe that," Marina said quietly. "I didn't know things had gone that far for you."

"They had. I love him and now he's gone."

She began to cry again.

"Oh, Willow." Marina hugged her close. "We'll figure

this out. I'll kidnap him and we'll keep him weak and thirsty until he realizes he needs you in his life."

Willow hiccupped a small laugh. "If he was naked, I could get into that plan."

"I'm sorry," Marina whispered into her hair. "I'm so sorry. What do you want to do? Eat ice cream? Scream? Throw some plates? Come up with a way to win him back?"

If only, Willow thought. "I can't win him back. I can't make him want to be with me. He has to decide that on his own and I don't think he's going to."

It was dark when Kane returned to the house. He walked inside and heard...nothing.

The cats were gone, the plants were gone, and Willow was gone. He walked through the rooms and saw that despite taking everything he'd asked, she'd still left her mark.

His magazines were fanned out in a circle, which she always did while she was talking on the phone. There was food in the refrigerator and cookies in the large red strawberry cookie jar she'd bought. In the bathroom, the sweet scent of her perfume lingered.

He saw a white shirt hanging on the back of the door. It was his, so she'd left it, but it was the one she wore instead of a robe. He picked it up and held it in his hand, as if he could still touch her.

But he couldn't. She was gone. Just like he wanted.

He returned to the living room and waited for the peace that silence always brought. But tonight there was only the restless need to keep moving. He changed into workout clothes and decided to get in another hour at the gym. Maybe then he would sleep.

It was nearly midnight when he finally crawled into bed.

He was exhausted and yet he couldn't close his eyes. The silence was too loud.

Finally he got up and retrieved the shirt she'd used from the back of the bathroom door, then laid it out next to him. Stupid, he thought. No, beyond stupid. Pathetic.

And then he got it. He missed her. He, who had always prided himself on never missing anyone, missed her more than he could say.

Twelve

Kane gathered his keys and briefcase, then walked to his front door. But before he could open it, someone knocked.

For a second he did nothing. He stood on the tile and listened to the sound of his heart beating. He knew what he wanted, what he hoped, what he could never allow. Willow. But when he pulled open the door, Todd stood there.

"I'm glad I caught you," his boss said. "My car's acting up. Can I get a ride into the office with you? The dealer's going to come pick up my car and they'll deliver a loaner later this morning."

The disappointment was as real and fast as a gunshot. He wanted to howl to the heavens, to demand it be her. But after what he'd said, why would she bother?

"No problem," he told Todd. "I was on my way out."

"Good. I don't see Willow's car. Has she already left?"

"She's gone. We're not seeing each other anymore."

Todd raised his eyebrows. "I didn't know. I thought you two were getting along. That everything was great."

Kane hit the button to unlock his car, then stowed his briefcase in the backseat.

"I won't ask what happened." Todd climbed into the passenger seat. "God knows I'm avoiding women these days. Ruth has been on me until I finally agreed to a date with Marina. What the hell was I thinking?"

Kane didn't have an answer and he didn't want to talk about Marina. She reminded him of Willow and thinking about Willow made him hurt in ways he'd never imagined possible.

She'd changed him, he thought grimly. Silence and solitude had always been his refuge. He'd needed to be alone. Now the evenings and even his life stretched out endlessly before him. It was blank and empty and cold.

But how to change that? Give in? Care? And then what, he asked himself as he turned right. If he let her get close, let her get inside, where would he have to go? How could he protect himself?

"What's wrong with your car?" he asked as a way to distract himself and Todd. Discussing anything was preferable to talking about any of the Nelson sisters.

"Not sure. It just wouldn't start. It's only a few months old. Strange."

Something clicked in the back of Kane's mind. "Did it make a noise at all?"

"Sort of a raspy growl. It turned over a couple of times and went dead."

"You haven't pissed anyone off lately, have you?"

Todd looked at him. "You think it's more than just a car not starting?"

"I don't know. Do you have the dealership's number with you?" Kane asked.

"Sure."

"Call them and tell them not to bother picking up the car. That you'll have it dropped off later. I'll get a guy I know to go by and look it over first. Just in case."

Todd swore. "I don't like the sound of that."

"Better to be safe than—"

Something big and fast moving rammed into them from the side, pushing them into oncoming traffic on the busy street. Kane's car skidded, but he easily kept control. Even as he steered back into the correct lane and avoided an accident, he scanned for the attacker while pulling his gun out of its holster.

He saw it. A silver import. It headed for them again. The sun worked against him, keeping him from seeing the driver.

"Brace yourself," he told Todd, then braked suddenly.

Their attacker shot past them. Kane took aim but before he could pull the trigger, he felt something. A flash of information he couldn't process, a hunch, whatever, followed by the clear and unwelcome realization that Willow wouldn't want him to kill anyone.

He swore, took aim again, only to watch the car crash into light pole and come to a stop.

He drove to the side of the road and called 911. He was out of the car and heading for the driver as the operator picked up. He gave the location of the accident and described what happened automatically, all the while wondering what else she'd changed inside of him and how he would ever find his way back to who he had been.

Kane finished with the police a little after ten-thirty that morning. His car would need some serious body work but it was still drivable. He was about to climb inside when a paramedic stopped him.

"Do we need to look at you?" he asked Kane.

"I'm good. Had my seat belt on."

"So did the kid. Otherwise he'd be dead now."

Kane eyed the totaled wreck being pulled onto a flatbed tow truck. "The police said he is a teenager. That he passed out."

The paramedic nodded. "He is seventeen, a senior in high school. According to his mom, he's a diabetic. Apparently he screwed up his injection this morning and went into insulin shock. When he rammed into you, he was so out of it, I doubt he knew he was driving. You handled the situation like a pro. If you'd let him hit you again, I don't think he would have survived the impact."

The paramedic left.

Kane stood by his car and sucked in a breath. A seventeen-year-old boy. What if he'd shot the kid? Under the circumstances, he wouldn't have been charged. The concealed weapon was legal and Kane was a trained professional. But that would have been cold comfort to the kid's family. And to himself.

Six months ago, he would have fired without a second thought. Today he hadn't been able to. And he knew why.

That night Kane sat alone in the dark and got drunk.

He didn't usually drink to excess, but after today, he figured he'd earned it. Maybe with enough liquor in his body, he could finally forget what he'd almost done that morning. Maybe he could forget about Willow, about how much he missed her.

Maybe. But he had his doubts.

* * *

Willow looked at her boss. "Beverly, it's only been a month."

"I know." Beverly grinned at her. "You should just nod and say thank you."

"Thank you," Willow said and meant it. She'd just gotten a raise and it was a big one.

"You're a find," the other woman told her. "You're a natural with both the plants and the customers. That's rare. Usually it's one or the other. With you to help me, I can expand the way I've always wanted to. You're organized and creative and easy to work with. I don't want anyone to steal you away."

The compliments were flowing so fast, Willow could barely absorb them all. Still, she liked the feeling of pride that welled up inside of her.

"I don't want to be stolen," she admitted. "I love working here. Thanks for the raise."

"You're welcome."

"I'm going to get back to the exotics."

"Great. Do whatever you've been doing. They've never looked better."

Willow waved and walked to the rear of the nursery. She felt good—better than good. If not for the giant hole where her heart used to be, she'd be positively floating.

An hour later, she was elbow deep in soil and nutrients for the growth mixture she'd started experimenting with.

"Hello, Willow."

The low male voice could have caused a shiver in her belly, except it wasn't one she recognized. She turned and saw a tall, handsome, well-dressed man standing inside the greenhouse tent.

Hmm—dark hair, dark eyes and a slightly more than passing resemblance to Julie's fiancé, Ryan.

She sat back on her heels. "Let me guess," she said. "The infamous Todd Aston the Third."

"We meet at last. I understand you want to give me a piece of your mind."

"Is that why you're here?"

"No, but I'll listen if it will make you feel better."

"It won't." Maybe at one time she'd wanted to yell at Todd, but not anymore. She had bigger worries sucking at her energy. "Julie and Ryan are getting married. That's what's important to me."

"Me, too."

She stared at him.

"Don't look surprised," he told her. "Ryan and I have been friends all our lives. I care about him. I want whatever makes him happy and that's Julie."

"Cheap talk."

He gave her a slight smile. "We'll have this conversation again in ten years and then you'll have to believe me."

Ten years? Right. Todd and Ryan were cousins. So when Ryan became a part of the family, Todd was going to be tagging along. Did that mean there would be shared functions? Would she run into Kane at one of them?

The thought was both thrilling and exquisitely painful. To see him but not be with him would be torture. Yet the thought of never seeing him again was worse.

"Are you doing all right?" Todd asked. "I know about the breakup."

Was that the reason for his unexpected visit? Did Kane want an update? Somehow she doubted that. "I'm getting by."

"Kane isn't. He's in pretty bad shape."

Her first instinct was to run to him and try to make

things better. But he'd made it clear he didn't want her help or even her.

She stood and brushed off her jeans. "I'm sorry to hear that, but it's not my business."

"I don't know what happened between the two of you, but I've known Kane for a few years now. He's a great guy. He's careful about who he gets involved with." Todd frowned. "You're the first girlfriend I can remember in his life. So maybe you could cut him a break and give him a second chance."

She stared at Todd. "You think *I* ended things?"

"Didn't you? The way he's been acting, I figured…"

"Sorry, no. He left me. He made it incredibly clear that he wanted nothing to do with me. We didn't have a fight, we didn't disagree, he simply decided it was over."

Saying the words made her ache inside, but there was no point in hiding from the truth.

Todd shifted awkwardly. "I didn't know."

"Now you do." She faced him. "I love Kane. I told him and I think he couldn't handle it. I wish things were different, that he were different, but they are what they are. He doesn't need a second chance with me. He needs to figure out whether he's interested in a first one."

"I'm sorry."

"I'll survive. I come from a long line of strong women." She thought about her family. "Strong women who sometimes make foolish choices when it comes to men."

"If there's anything I can do…"

"There isn't, but thanks." She put her hands on her hips. "Wait a minute. You came here to make things right with me and Kane—why would you bother?"

"I told you. I wanted to help my friend."

"So you're not totally evil?"

"Is that a question and if so, do you expect me to answer it?"

"I guess not. But you surprise me. You were so icky about Julie and Ryan."

"I was *not* icky and I thought Julie was in it for the money."

"She would never do that."

"I know that now."

"You should have given her the benefit of the doubt. It's the right thing to do."

"Not if you have my past."

"Oh, I see. So you're going to punish every woman you meet because you had the poor judgment to pick badly in the past. That's something to look forward to. I'll be sure to tell Marina."

Todd looked both pained and amused by her comments. "You know about our date."

"Oh, yeah. We're all counting the hours."

One corner of his mouth twitched. "Is she more like you or more like Julie?"

"You'll have to figure that out for yourself. But I will tell you that she's incredibly smart, so don't try any of your smarmy crap on her."

"Smarmy crap?" He grinned. "I'll remember that. Leave the smarmy crap at home."

She hated that he was amused. "You know what I mean."

"I do." His humor faded. "It was delightful to meet you, Willow. I'm sorry Kane was moronic enough to let you go. I think you would have been good for him."

She nodded, mostly because her eyes had started burning and she knew where that road led.

She maintained control until Todd had left, then she let the tears fall. She wanted to believe that his visit meant something, but how could it? Kane hadn't sent him. She would bet he didn't even know about Todd stopping by.

Todd had said Kane was in bad shape. Did the fact that he was hurting mean anything? Would he want to fix the problem or simply muscle through it?

Despite everything, she wanted to go to him and hold him until he felt better. But she wouldn't. She couldn't force the man to love her and she was no longer interested in someone who only saw her as a convenience. She'd thought she meant more, but she'd been wrong.

That night Willow curled up in a corner of her sofa and tried to get interested in the movie she'd rented. It was a comedy and it seemed to be pretty funny, but none of the jokes were making her laugh. Maybe because she hurt too much inside.

She reached for the remote control, thinking she would just go to bed and try the movie another time, when she heard an odd noise outside. It sounded like scratching. Or whining. Or both.

She listened and heard the sound again.

She crossed to her front door and pulled it open. A black, fluffy, furry, adorable puppy stared up at her, then yipped.

Delighted, she dropped to her knees. The puppy plunged into her arms and began licking her face.

"Who are you?" she asked as she laughed and tried to hold on to the wiggling buddle of kisses. "Where did you come from? Are you lost?"

"He's not the one who's lost," Kane said, stepping out of the shadows.

Her heart froze. She actually felt it stop midbeat. Her breath caught in her throat and she momentarily lost her hold on the puppy who used her inattention to lunge forward and knock her onto her back.

"Okay, that's enough." Kane stepped forward and grabbed the puppy under one arm. He used his free hand to pull her to her feet. "He gets kind of rowdy."

"I can see that."

She didn't know what to think, what to feel. "Why are you here?"

"Can we come in? He should be okay. He just had his way with a couple of your rosebushes out front, so I think he's safe on carpet for a few minutes."

The only man she'd ever loved, the man who had so clearly rejected her, was talking about whether or not a puppy would pee on her rug?

She stepped back and let them both in. Kane set down the puppy, who ran to her and began licking her bare feet.

She dropped to her knees and gathered the puppy close. "Does he have a name?" she asked because talking about the dog was a whole lot safer than talking about anything else.

She wanted to believe that Kane's presence here meant something, but she wasn't sure. And she hurt too much to hope.

"Not yet. I thought you'd want to name him." Kane crouched next to her. "He's yours. I bought him for you. But he lives with me, so if you want him, you're going to have to come back to me."

She swallowed. Okay, sure, now there was hope, but there was also fear and a broken heart. "You want me back?"

"Want?" He shook his head. "*Want* is such a small word, Willow. I thought I knew what I wanted. Solitude. My peaceful world. I had it all planned out. I was careful—I never got involved. I knew what caring meant and I wasn't going to be a sucker twice. No one got in, ever. Until you."

The hope got a little bigger and brighter. Her breathing quickened.

"I thought I wanted to live on an island somewhere, by myself. I thought I wanted what I had. I did—until I met you. Everything changed after that. Now I want noise and confusion and conversation and laughter. I want candles and plants and food and your mess everywhere."

"I'm not that messy."

He smiled, then reached out and stroked her cheek. The puppy licked them both. "I'm sorry. I'm sorry for what I said and I'm sorry for how I hurt you. The pain in your eyes, pain that I put there, haunts me. I miss you, Willow. I don't just want you. I ache for you. I need you with a desperation that leaves me weak. You made me into a man I never thought I could be. You have changed me as fundamentally as a man can change. It took me awhile to figure all that out. I've never been in love before, so I didn't recognize the signs."

Love? Love!

She released the puppy and reached for Kane. "So you're saying…"

"I love you." He gathered her close and held on tight. "I love you. For always. Through sickness and in health and through babies and houses and whatever else happens. If you can forgive me. If you still love me."

She pulled back and stared at him. "What? Because you thought I might just fall out of love with you?"

She saw the fear in his eyes and knew he'd been afraid of just that. "I hurt you," he said. "I was cruel. I can't excuse what I did. I can only promise I'll never do it again."

He was not a man who gave his word lightly. She trusted him to love her for always, just as she trusted him to be there for her and their children and pets and whatever else might enter their lives.

"I do love you," she said.

"Will you marry me?"

She smiled. "Yes. Do we get to keep Jasmine?"

He grinned. "Of course."

"And at least one of the kittens?"

He sighed. "It's your life, too. You get to decide."

"I hope they like Bobo. He's got some big paws on him. I'm thinking he'll get to fifty or sixty pounds."

He closed his eyes and groaned. "We're not calling the dog Bobo."

"Muffin?"

"It's a boy, Willow. Can he have a little dignity? What about Blackie?"

"Oh, that's original. I'm thinking he looks like a Stan."

Kane groaned.

Willow curled up in his arms. "We're going to need a bigger house. Not that I don't love Todd, but do we have to live that close?"

"We'll move. And since when do you love Todd?"

"It's family love. Don't worry. He's not a threat."

"Good to know. We'll buy a bigger house on its own lot."

"With a yard," she said.

"And a garden."

"Ooh, yeah. A big garden. And a big bedroom, because we'll be spending lots of time in it."

"I like the way you think." He stared into her eyes. "I love you, Willow. You've changed everything for me."

"I rescued you." She grinned. "Although I'm retired now. The world will have to get by without my rescuing skills. Except for plants and pets. We're going to have kids, right?"

He began unbuttoning her blouse. "Of course."

"As many as I want?"

"You're the one who has to carry them." He removed her blouse.

She glanced over his shoulder and saw Stan had collapsed on a cushion by the sofa.

"We'll have to be very quiet," she whispered.

Kane stood, then picked her up in his arms and carried her down the hall. "I was thinking we'd just leave the room."

"That works, too."

* * * * *

Don't miss the conclusion to
THE MILLION DOLLAR CATCH,
Susan Mallery's sexy new miniseries.
And find out if Todd Aston the Third really is
THE ULTIMATE MILLIONAIRE.
On sale January 2007
Wherever Silhouette Books are sold.

Turn the page for a sneak peek at
Susan's latest novel,
SIZZLING.
Available from HQN Books in January 2007.

CHAPTER ONE

Until 6:45 on that Thursday morning, women had always loved Reid Buchanan.

They'd started leaving notes in his locker long before he'd figured out the opposite sex could be anything but annoying. During his sophomore year of high school, his hormones had kicked in and he'd become aware of all the possibilities. Over spring break of that year, Misty O'Connell, a senior, had seduced him in her parents' basement on a rainy Seattle afternoon, during an MTV Real World marathon.

He'd adored women from that moment on and they had returned the affection. Until today, when he casually turned the page in the morning paper and saw his picture next to an article with the headline Fame, Absolutely. Fortune, You Bet. But Good in Bed? Not So Much.

Reid nearly spit out his coffee as he jerked to his feet and stared at the page. He blinked, then rubbed his eyes and read the headline again.

Not good in bed? NOT GOOD IN BED?

"She's crazy," he muttered, knowing the author had to be a woman he'd dated and dumped. This was about revenge. About getting back at him and humiliating him in public. Because he was good in bed, dammit. Better than good.

He made women scream on a regular basis. They clawed his back—he had the scars to prove it. They stole into his hotel room at night when he was on the road, they begged, they followed him home and offered him anything if he would just sleep with them again.

He was better than good. He was a god!

He was also completely and totally screwed, he thought as he sank back into his chair and scanned the article. Sure enough, the author had gone out with him. It had been one night of what she described as nearly charming conversation, almost-funny stories from his past and a so-so couple of hours naked. It was all couched in "don't sue me" language. Things like "Just one reporter's opinion" and "Maybe it's just me, but…"

He studied the name of the reporter, but it meant nothing. Not even a whisper of a memory. There wasn't a picture, so he grabbed his laptop and went online to the paper's Web site. Under the bio section he found a photo.

He studied the average-looking brunette and had a vague recollection of something. Okay, yeah, so maybe he'd slept with her, but just because he couldn't remember what had happened didn't mean it hadn't been incredible.

But along with the fuzzy memories was the idea that he'd gone out with her during the play-offs, when his former team had been fighting for a chance to make the World Series and he'd been back in Seattle, in his first year of retirement. He'd been bitter and angry about being out of the game. He might have been drunk.

"I was thinking about baseball instead of her. So sue me," he muttered as he read the article again.

Deep, soul-shriveling embarrassment chilled him. Instead of calling him a bastard to all of her friends, this woman had chosen to humiliate him in public. How the hell was he supposed to fight back? In the courts? He'd been around long enough to know he didn't have a case, and even if he did, how was he supposed to win? Parade a bunch of women around who would swear he made the earth move just by kissing them?

While he kind of liked that idea, he knew it wouldn't make a difference. He'd been a famous baseball player once, and there was nothing the public liked more than to see the mighty fall.

His friends would read this. His family would read this. Everyone he knew in Seattle would read it. He could only imagine what would happen when he walked into the Downtown Sports Bar today.

At least it was local, he thought grimly. Contained. He wouldn't have to deal with hearing from his old baseball buddies.

The phone rang. He grabbed it.

"Hello."

"Mr. Buchanan? Reid? Hi. I'm a producer here at Access Hollywood. I was wondering if you'd like to make a comment on the article in the Seattle paper this morning. The one about—"

"I know what it's about," he growled.

"Oh, good." The young woman on the other end of the phone giggled. "How about an interview? I could have a crew there this morning. I'm sure you want to tell your side of things."

He hung up and swore. Access Hollywood? Already?

The phone rang again. He pulled the plug and thought about throwing it against the wall, but the damn phone wasn't responsible for this disaster.

His cell rang. He hesitated before picking it up. The caller ID showed a familiar number. A friend from Atlanta. He exhaled with relief. Okay, this call he could take.

"Hey, Tommy. How's it going?"

"Reid, buddy. Have you seen it? The article? It's every-where. Total bummer. And for the record—dude, too much information."

If Lori Johnston had believed in previous lives, she would have wondered if in one of hers she'd been a general, or some other kind of tactical expert. There was nothing she liked more than taking a few unrelated elements, mixing them together and creating the perfect solution to a problem.

This morning she had to deal with hospital equipment arriving the day *after* it was supposed to and a catering service delivery with every single entrée wrong. In her free time, she had her new patient to meet and safely delivered home, assuming the ambulance driver wasn't late. Where other people would be screaming and threatening, Lori felt only energized. She would meet this challenge as she met all others and she would be victorious.

The deliverymen finished assembling the state-of-the-art hospital bed and stepped back for her inspection. She stretched out on the mattress to check for bumps and low-spots. What might just be annoying to someone healthy could be impossible to endure when one had a broken hip.

When the mattress passed inspection, she worked the controls.

"There's a squeak when I raise the bed," she said. "Can you fix that?"

The men shared an exasperated glance, but she didn't care. Trying to get comfortable while in pain was bad enough, but an annoying noise could make things worse.

She checked out the table on wheels, and it was fine, as were the wheelchair and the walker.

While they dealt with the squeak, Lori hurried into the

massive kitchen where the catering staff sorted through the meals they'd brought.

"The chili?" a woman in a white uniform asked.

"Has to go." Lori pointed to the list she'd posted on the refrigerator. "This is a woman who is in her seventies. She's had a heart attack and surgery on a broken hip. She's on medication. I said tasty, but not spicy. We want to encourage her to eat, but she may still have stomach issues from all the medication. She doesn't need to lose weight, so that's not a problem. Healthy, tempting dishes. Not chili, not sushi, nothing fancy."

She'd been so specific on the phone, too, she thought with minor exasperation.

"You could beat them. That would get their attention."

That voice. Lori didn't have to turn around to know who was standing in the doorway of the kitchen. Amused, no doubt, because God forbid he should have an actual meaningful thought or do something constructive.

She braced herself for the impact of the dark, knowing eyes, the handsome-but-just-shy-of-too-handsome face and the casual slouch that should have annoyed the heck out of her, but instead made her want to melt like a twelve-year-old at a Jesse McCartney concert.

Reid Buchanan was everything she disliked in a man. He'd always had it easy so nothing had value. Women threw themselves at him. He'd had a brilliant career playing baseball, although she'd never followed sports and didn't know any details. And he'd never once in his entire life bothered with a woman as ordinary as her.

"Don't you have something better to do than just show up and annoy me?" she asked as she turned toward him.

The impact of his physical presence was immediate. She found it difficult to breathe, let alone think.

"Annoying you is an unexpected bonus," he said, "but not the reason I'm here. My grandmother's coming home today."

"I know that. I arranged it."

"I thought I'd stop by to visit her."

"I'm sure knowing you stopped by four hours before she was due home will brighten her day so much that the healing process will be cut in half."

She pushed past him, ignoring the quick brush of her arm against his and the humiliating burst of heat that ignited inside of her. She was pathetic. No, she was worse than pathetic—one day she would grow enough to achieve pathetic and that would be a victory.

"She won't be here until this afternoon?" he asked as he followed her back into the library.

"Unfortunately, no. But it was thrilling to see you. So sorry you can't stay."

He leaned against the door frame in the room. He did that a lot. He must know how good he looked doing it, Lori thought grimly. No doubt he practiced at home.

She knew Reid was shallow and selfish and only interested in women as perfect as himself, so why was she attracted to him? She was intelligent. She should know better. And she did…in her head. It was the rest of her that was the problem.

She was a total and complete cliché—a smart, average-looking woman pining after the unobtainable. The bookstores probably contained an entire shelf of self-help books dedicated to her condition. If she believed in self-help books, she could go get herself healed.

As it was, she was stuck with enduring.

"Don't you have to go away?" she asked.

"For now, but I'll be back."

"I'll count the hours."

"You do that." He stayed where he was, apparently un-movable.

"What?" she asked. "Are we waiting for something?"

He smiled, a slow, sexy smile that caused her heart to actually skip a beat. It was a new low.

"You don't read the paper, do you?" he asked.

"No. I go running in the morning and I listen to music."

The smile brightened. "Good. I'll see you later."

"You could wait until the evening nurse shows up and visit then. Wouldn't that be a great plan?"

"But then you'd miss me. Snarling at me is the best part of your day. Bye, Lori."

And then he was gone.

* * * * *

*Experience entertaining women's fiction for
every woman who has wondered
"what's next?" in her life.
Turn the page for a sneak preview of
a new book from* Harlequin NEXT,
*WHY IS MURDER ON THE MENU, ANYWAY?
by Stevi Mittman.*

On sale December 2006, wherever books are sold.

Ambience is everything. Imagine eating a foie gras at a luncheonette counter or a side of coleslaw at Le Cirque. It's not a matter of food but one of atmosphere. Remember that when planning your dining room design.
—Tips from *Teddi.com*

"Now that's the kind of man you should be looking for," my mother, the self-appointed keeper of my shelf life stamp, says. She points with her fork at a man in the corner of the Steak-Out Restaurant, a dive I've just been hired to redecorate. Making this restaurant look four-star will be hard, but not half as hard as getting through lunch without strangling the woman across the table from me. "*He* would make a good husband."

"Oh, you can tell that from across the room?" I ask, wondering how it is she can forget that when we had trouble getting rid of my last husband, she shot him. "Besides being ten minutes away from death if he actually eats all that steak, he's twenty years too old for me and—shallow woman that I am—twenty pounds too heavy.

Besides, I am *so* not looking for another husband here. I'm looking to design a new image for this place, looking for some sense of ambience, some feeling, something I can build a proposal on for them."

My mother studies the man in the corner, tilting her head, the better to gauge his age, I suppose. I think she's grimacing, but with all the Botox and Restylane injected into that face, it's hard to tell. She takes another bite of her steak, chews slowly so that I don't miss the fact that the steak is a poor cut and tougher than it should be. "You're concentrating on the wrong kind of proposal," she says finally. "Just look at this place, Teddi. It's a dive. There are hardly any other diners. What does *that* tell you about the food?"

"That they cater to a dinner crowd and it's lunchtime," I tell her.

I don't know what I was thinking bringing her here with me. I suppose I thought it would be better than eating alone. There really are days when my common sense goes on vacation. Clearly, this is one of them. I mean really, did I not resolve less than three weeks ago that I would not let my mother get to me anymore?

What good are New Year's resolutions, anyway?

Mario approaches the man's table and my mother studies him while they converse. Eventually Mario leaves the table with a huff, after which the diner glances up and meets my mother's gaze. I think she's smiling at him. That or she's got indigestion. They size each other up.

I concentrate on making sketches in my notebook and try to ignore the fact that my mother is flirting. At nearly seventy, she's developed an unhealthy interest in members of the opposite sex to whom she isn't married.

According to my father, who has broken the TMI rule and given me Too Much Information, she has no interest in sex with him. Better, I suppose, to be clued in on what they aren't doing in the bedroom than have to hear what they might be doing.

"He's not so old," my mother says, noticing that I have barely touched the Chinese chicken salad she warned me not to get. "He's got about as many years on you as you have on your little cop friend."

She does this to make me crazy. I know it, but it works all the same. "Drew Scoones is not my little 'friend.' He's a detective with whom I—"

"Screwed around," my mother says. I must look shocked, because my mother laughs at me and asks if I think she doesn't know the "lingo."

What I thought she didn't know was that Drew and I actually tangled in the sheets. And, since it's possible she's just fishing, I sidestep the issue and tell her that Drew is just a couple of years younger than me and that I don't need reminding. I dig into my salad with renewed vigor, determined to show my mother that Chinese chicken salad in a steak place was not the stupid choice it's proving to be.

After a few more minutes of my picking at the wilted leaves on my plate, the man my mother has me nearly engaged to pays his bill and heads past us toward the back of the restaurant. I watch my mother take in his shoes, his suit and the diamond pinkie ring that seems to be cutting off the circulation in his little finger.

"Such nice hands," she says after the man is out of sight. "Manicured." She and I both stare at my hands. I have two popped acrylics that are being held on at weird angles by bandages. My cuticles are ragged and there's marker decorating my right hand from measuring carelessly when I did a drawing for a customer.

Twenty minutes later she's disappointed that he managed to leave the restaurant without our noticing. He will join the list of the ones I let get away. I will hear about him twenty years from now when—according to my mother—my children will be grown and I will still be single, living pathetically alone with several dogs and cats.

After my ex, that sounds good to me.

The waitress tells us that our meal has been taken care of by the management and, after thanking Mario, the owner, complimenting him on the wonderful meal and assuring him that once I have redecorated his place people will be flocking here in droves (I actually use those words and ignore my mother when she rolls her eyes), my mother and I head for the restroom.

My father—unfortunately not with us today—has the patience of a saint. He got it over the years of living with my mother. She, perhaps as a result, figures he has the patience for both of them, and feels justified having none. For her, no rules apply, and a little thing like a picture of a man on the door to a public restroom is certainly no barrier to using the john. In all fairness, it does seem silly to stand and wait for the ladies' room if no one is using the men's room.

Still, it's the idea that rules don't apply to her, signs don't apply to her, conventions don't apply to her. She knocks on the door to the men's room. When no one answers she gestures to me to go in ahead. I tell her that I can certainly wait for the ladies' room to be free and she shrugs and goes in herself.

Not a minute later there is a bloodcurdling scream from behind the men's room door.

"Mom!" I yell. "Are you all right?"

Mario comes running over, the waitress on his heels.

Two customers head our way while my mother continues to scream.

I try the door, but it is locked. I yell for her to open it
and she fumbles with the knob. When she finally
manages to unlock and open it, she is white behind her
two streaks of blush, but she is on her feet and appears
shaken but not stirred.

"What happened?" I ask her. So do Mario and the
waitress and the few customers who have migrated to the
back of the place.

She points toward the bathroom and I go in, thinking
it serves her right for using the men's room. But I see
nothing amiss.

She gestures toward the stall, and, like any self-respect-
ing and suspicious woman, I poke the door open with one
finger, expecting the worst.

What I find is worse than the worst.

The husband my mother picked out for me is sitting on
the toilet. His pants are puddled around his ankles, his
hands are hanging at his sides. Pinned to his chest is some
sort of Health Department certificate.

Oh, and there is a large, round, bloodless bullet hole
between his eyes.

Four Nassau County police officers are securing the
area, waiting for the detectives and crime scene personnel
to show up. They are trying, though not very hard, to
comfort my mother, who in another era would be considered to be suffering from the vapors. Less tactful in the
twenty-first century, I'd say she was losing it. That is, if I
didn't know her better, know she was milking it for everything it was worth.

My mother loves attention. As it begins to flag, she

swoons and claims to feel faint. Despite four No Smoking signs, my mother insists it's all right for her to light up because, after all, she's in shock. Not to mention that signs, as we know, don't apply to her.

When asked not to smoke, she collapses mournfully in a chair and lets her head loll to the side, all without mussing her hair.

Eventually, the detectives show up to find the four patrolmen all circled around her, debating whether to administer CPR, smelling salts or simply call the paramedics. I, however, know just what will snap her to attention.

"Detective Scoones," I say loudly. My mother parts the sea of cops.

"We have to stop meeting like this," he says lightly to me, but I can feel him checking me over with his eyes, making sure I'm all right while pretending not to care.

"What have you got in those pants?" my mother asks him, coming to her feet and staring at his crotch accusingly. "*Baydar?* Everywhere we Bayers are, you turn up. You don't expect me to buy that this is a coincidence, I hope."

Drew tells my mother that it's nice to see her, too, and asks if it's his fault that her daughter seems to attract disasters.

Charming to be made to feel like the bearer of a plague. He asks how I am.

"Just peachy," I tell him. "I seem to be making a habit of finding dead bodies, my mother is driving me crazy and the catering hall I booked two freakin' years ago for Dana's bat mitzvah has just been shut down by the Board of Health!"

"Glad to see your luck's finally changing," he says, giving me a quick squeeze around the shoulders before turning his attention to the patrolmen, asking what they've got, whether they've taken any statements, moved anything, all the sort of stuff you see on TV, without any of the drama. That is, if you don't count my mother's threats to faint every few minutes when she senses no one's paying attention to her.

Mario tells his waitstaff to bring everyone espresso, which I decline because I'm wired enough. Drew pulls him aside and a minute later I'm handed a cup of coffee that smells divinely of Kahlúa.

The man knows me well. Too well.

His partner, whom I've met once or twice, says he'll interview the kitchen staff. Drew asks Mario if he minds if he takes statements from the patrons first and gets to him and the waitstaff afterward.

"No, no," Mario tells him. "Do the patrons first." Drew raises his eyebrow at me like he wants to know if I get the double entendre. I try to look bored.

"What is it with you and murder victims?" he asks me when we sit down at a table in the corner.

I search them out so that I can see you again, I almost say, but I'm afraid it will sound desperate instead of sarcastic.

My mother, lighting up and daring him with a look to tell her not to, reminds him that *she* was the one to find the body.

Drew asks what happened *this time*. My mother tells him how the man in the john was "taken" with me, couldn't take his eyes off me and blatantly flirted with both of us. To his credit, Drew doesn't laugh, but his smirk is undeniable to the trained eye. And I've had my eye trained on him for nearly a year now.

"While he was noticing you," he asks me, "did *you* notice anything about him? Was he waiting for anyone? Watching for anything?"

I tell him that he didn't appear to be waiting or watching. That he made no phone calls, was fairly intent on eating and did, indeed, flirt with my mother. This last bit Drew takes with a grain of salt, which was the way it was intended.

"And he had a short conversation with Mario," I tell him. "I think he might have been unhappy with the food, though he didn't send it back."

Drew asks what makes me think he was dissatisfied, and I tell him that the discussion seemed acrimonious and that Mario looked distressed when he left the table. Drew makes a note and says he'll look into it and asks about anyone else in the restaurant. Did I see anyone who didn't seem to belong, anyone who was watching the victim, anyone looking suspicious?

"Besides my mother?" I ask him, and Mom huffs and blows her cigarette smoke in my direction.

I tell him that there were several deliveries, the kitchen staff going in and out the back door to grab a smoke. He stops me and asks what I was doing checking out the back door of the restaurant.

Proudly—because, while he was off forgetting me, dropping by only once in a while to say hi to Jesse, my son, or drop something by for one of my daughters that he thought they might like, I was getting on with my life—I tell him that I'm decorating the place.

He looks genuinely impressed. "Commercial customers? That's great," he says. Okay, that's what he *ought* to say. What he actually says is "Whatever pays the bills."

"Howard Rosen, the famous restaurant critic, got her the job," my mother says. "You met him—the good-looking, distinguished gentleman with the *real* job, something to be proud of. I guess you've never read his reviews in *Newsday*."

Drew, without missing a beat, tells her that Howard's reviews are on the top of his list, as soon as he learns how to read.

"I only meant—" my mother starts, but both of us assure her that we know just what she meant.

"So," Drew says. "Deliveries?"

I tell him that Mario would know better than I, but that I saw vegetables come in, maybe fish and linens.

"This is the second restaurant job Howard's got her," my mother tells Drew.

"At least she's getting *something* out of the relationship," he says.

"If he were here," my mother says, ignoring the insinuation, "he'd be comforting her instead of interrogating her. He'd be making sure we're both all right after such an ordeal."

"I'm sure he would," Drew agrees, then looks me in the eyes as if he's measuring my tolerance for shock. Quietly he adds, "But then maybe he doesn't know just what strong stuff your daughter's made of."

It's the closest thing to a tender moment I can expect from Drew Scoones. My mother breaks the spell. "She gets that from me," she says.

Both Drew and I take a minute, probably to pray that's all I inherited from her.

"I'm just trying to save you some time and effort," my mother tells him. "My money's on Howard."

Drew withers her with a look and mutters something that sounds suspiciously like "fool's gold." Then he excuses himself to go back to work.

I catch his sleeve and ask if it's all right for us to leave. He says sure, he knows where we live. I say goodbye to Mario. I assure him that I will have some sketches for him in a few days, all the while hoping that this murder doesn't cancel his redecorating plans. I need the money desperately, the alternative being borrowing from my parents and being strangled by the strings.

My mother is strangely quiet all the way to her house. She doesn't tell me what a loser Drew Scoones is—despite his good looks—and how I was obviously drooling over him. She doesn't ask me where Howard is taking me tonight or warn me not to tell my father about what happened because he will worry about us both and no doubt insist we see our respective psychiatrists.

She fidgets nervously, opening and closing her purse over and over again.

"You okay?" I ask her. After all, she's just found a dead man on the toilet, and tough as she is that's got to be upsetting.

When she doesn't answer me I pull over to the side of the road.

"Mom?" She refuses to meet my eyes. "You want me to take you to see Dr. Cohen?"

She looks out the window as if she's just realized we're on Broadway in Woodmere. "Aren't we near Marvin's Jewelers?" she asks, pulling something out of her purse.

"What have you got, Mother?" I ask, prying open her fingers to find the murdered man's ring.

"It was on the sink," she says in answer to my dropped jaw. "I was going to get his name and address and have you return it to him so that he could ask you out. I thought it was a sign that the two of you were meant to be together."

"He's dead, Mom. You understand that, right?" I ask. You never can tell when my mother is fine and when she's in la-la land.

"Well, I didn't know that," she shouts at me. "Not at the time."

I ask why she didn't give it to Drew, realize that she wouldn't give Drew the time in a clock shop and add, "…or one of the other policemen?"

"For heaven's sake," she tells me. "The man is dead, Teddi, and I took his ring. How would that look?"

Before I can tell her it looks just the way it is, she pulls out a cigarette and threatens to light it.

"I mean, really," she says, shaking her head like it's my brains that are loose. "What does he need with it now?"

Silhouette®

nocturne™

**WAS HE HER SAVIOR
OR HER NIGHTMARE?**

HAUNTED
LISA CHILDS

Years ago, Ariel and her sisters were separated for
their own protection. Now the man who vowed
revenge on her family has resumed the hunt, and
Ariel must warn her sisters before it's too late.
The closer she comes to finding them, the more
secretive her fiancé becomes. Can she trust the man
she plans to spend eternity with? Or has he been
waiting for the perfect moment to destroy her?

On sale December 2006.

In February, expect MORE
from

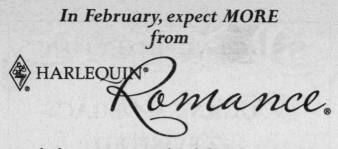

HARLEQUIN® *Romance*®

as it increases to six titles per month.

What's to come...

Rancher and Protector

Part of the

Western Weddings
miniseries

BY JUDY CHRISTENBERRY

The Boss's
Pregnancy Proposal

BY RAYE MORGAN

Don't miss February's
incredible line up of authors!

![Silhouette]

SPECIAL EDITION™

LOGAN'S LEGACY REVISITED

THE LOGAN FAMILY IS BACK WITH SIX NEW STORIES.

Beginning in January 2007 with

THE COUPLE MOST LIKELY TO

by

LILIAN DARCY

Tragedy drove them apart. Reunited eighteen years later, their attraction was once again undeniable. But had time away changed Jake Logan enough to let him face his fears and commit to the woman he once loved?

REQUEST YOUR FREE BOOKS!

2 FREE NOVELS PLUS 2 FREE GIFTS!

Silhouette®

Desire®

Passionate, Powerful, Provocative!

SDES06

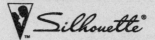

Don't miss
DAKOTA FORTUNES,
a six-book continuing series following
the Fortune family of South Dakota—
oil is in their blood and privilege
is their birthright.

This series kicks off with
USA TODAY bestselling author
PEGGY MORELAND'S
Merger of Fortunes
(SD #1771)
this January.

Other books in the series:
